F. Seamer

**Fluffy**

F. Seamer

**Fluffy**

ISBN/EAN: 9783741198847

Manufactured in Europe, USA, Canada, Australia, Japa

Cover: Foto ©Andreas Hilbeck / pixelio.de

Manufactured and distributed by brebook publishing software
(www.brebook.com)

F. Seamer

**Fluffy**

# FLUFFY.

# FLUFFY.

## By M. F. S.,

AUTHOR OF

"STORY OF THE LIFE OF ST. PAUL," "STORIES OF THE SAINTS,"
"STORIES OF HOLY LIVES," "STORIES OF MARTYR PRIESTS,"
"TOM'S CRUCIFIX, AND OTHER TALES," "CATHERINE HAMIL-
TON," "CATHERINE GROWN OLDER," ETC., ETC.

"Lord, when did we see Thee hungry, or thirsty, or a stranger,
or naked, or sick, or in prison, and did not minister unto Thee?
"Then He shall answer them, saying, 'Amen, I say unto you, as
long as you did it not to one of these least, neither did you do it
unto Me.'"

LONDON:
R. WASHBOURNE, 18 PATERNOSTER ROW.
1877.

𝔇𝔢𝔡𝔞𝔦𝔠𝔱𝔢𝔡

TO THE

## BROTHERS OF S. VINCENT DE PAUL,

WHO

HAVE ADDED TO THEIR MANY WORKS

OF CHARITY

THE PATRONAGE OF POOR AND FRIENDLESS BOYS.

# FLUFFY.

## CHAPTER I.

IT was dark and it was cold, though the month was only September.

Not a star glimmered in the sky, and heavy clouds obscured the moon, which had shone out so brightly only a night before.

A ragged dirty boy shivered in his thin old garments as he stood under the lamp-post at which the city omnibus filled with passengers all homeward bound. It was Fluffy's custom to stand there from about six to eight o'clock of evenings, poking his

*Echoes* into the faces of the gentlemen who
hurried by, regardless for the most part of
the ragged urchin, excepting as an impedi-
ment and obstruction on the footway.

Whether Fluffy had chosen an unfavour-
able stand I cannot say, but his sale of
papers was so small that he began to have
serious misgiving as to the popularity of
the *Echo,* coupled with the idea of going
in for some other paper when he saw his
way clear to the purchase.

On this particular night when the rain
fell so fast, chilling the poor boy through
and through, he had given up trying to effect
a sale, and only stood wearily against the
lamp-post, watching the tide of passers-by
without any particular reason for doing so.

Fluffy was an odd name, but he had
never known another during the eleven
years of his life.  You would scarcely have

believed him so old—he was so short and
so slight that he would have passed anywhere for a child of eight, unless, indeed,
you observed the sharp lines of his wan
little face, which had lost all the roundness
and all the innocence of childhood, if innocence there can be on the features or in the
heart of one whose earliest days have been
spent amidst the sights and sounds which
had always surrounded Fluffy.

" Well, young 'un, how's trade ?" said a
sharp, loud voice, which made Fluffy start.
It was a big, rough-looking boy, who once
upon a time had lodged in the same house,
but had gone off no one knew where, and
had developed from a ragged starving urchin
into a comfortably clad youth who did not
look like wanting a meal as badly as he *had*
needed one many and many a time in
Dockett's-buildings.

Now and then he encountered his former acquaintance, and seemed to find pleasure in Fluffy's miserable condition, for he always laughed long and loud when he made the little boy own to being cold or hungry.

"How's trade?" he said now, stopping short and surveying Fluffy by the light of the lamp beneath which he stood. "*You'll* never do any good at this sort of thing. There's too many of the regular newsboys to give *you* a chance."

Fluffy made no answer, for the good reason that none seemed expected; he only shifted from one leg to the other, and began a dreary little whistle.

"Come now, stop that row," said his friend. "You're cold, and you're hungry, and I'm most certain you've been a-cryin'."

"No I haven't," said Fluffy hotly; "it's the cold and the wet."

"Gammon," was the polite reply; "I know better. Why don't you try a different way of gettin' your livin'?"

"So I would if I knowed one," said Fluffy; and then with a sudden burst of courage, he added, "s'pose you was to tell me 'ow, as you *are* so mighty clever."

"So I might if you wasn't cheeky," responded the elder boy. "What'd you give if I was to put you up to *my* line of bisness?"

"I'd like that if it's a good one," said Fluffy. "You might tell a fellow, Joe."

"Oh yes I might, but s'pose I don't choose," said Joe Rogers. "Come, now, just you tell me if some of my old mates in the Buildin's don't want to find out what I'm a-doin'?"

"They say as your father's got into trouble," replied Fluffy.

The elder boy struck at him, but Fluffy

evaded the blow with a dexterity which
proved some practice. "Didn't I tell you
not to be cheeky?" said Joe. "I wasn't
sayin' anything about my father, was I?
If he's in trouble or not it's all the same to
me, for I don't want him. I'm on my own
hook, I am."

There was a moment's pause, during
which Fluffy looked half timidly and half
admiringly at the great rough lad before
him.

"I say, young 'un, s'pose I took you along
of me, and showed you 'ow to make a livin',
you'd like it, wouldn't you?"

"Yes," said Fluffy promptly. "Will
you, Joe?"

"No, I won't. I told you I wouldn't
help you if you was cheeky. I'm not goin'
to tell you nothin', so you can get home to
the Buildin's and your tipsy old granny, for

*you'll* not sell no more *Echoes* to-night," and laughing he went his way.

Perhaps Fluffy felt a shade of disappointment, but it was not much; he was too well used to his miserable life to have any strong hope of better days. Better days indeed! hadn't poor mother talked of them up to the very night when she died in the miserable half-underground kitchen which had been her home for a long while? "You wait a bit, Bill, and there'll be better days for us," she would say to her worthless husband, until he deserted her, and went off nobody knew where, and even then she had talked of them to Fluffy or any one who would listen.

And they never came — those better, brighter days—to the poor sick woman, nor did they seem very likely to dawn upon the miserable little boy she had left behind her.

He still lived in the damp room in Dockett's-buildings, with an old woman he
called granny, though she did not belong
to him. Some of the boys in the court
used to say that Fluffy had been "took for
rent," when his father deserted him and his
mother was dead; but however that might
be, some reason made the old woman keep
him instead of sending him to the workhouse as her neighbours advised her. The
house was her own, and let out by the
room to perhaps the worst set of all the
bad low people who herded together in
Dockett's-buildings. A wretched-looking
court it was. Always some quarrel or fight
going on unless it was early morning when
the inhabitants were apt to sleep, always the
half-dressed boys and girls playing on the
door-steps, the same crying babies, the same
idle slatternly women calling to their oppo-

site neighbours from either door or window, sometimes in friendly, but more often in abusive tones. As for windows, there was scarcely anything deserving the name, for in quarrels the panes were always smashed, and if one of the boys owed a grudge anywhere, what was easier than to throw a stone, and be rewarded by the pleasure of the sound of broken glass, and some angry voice denouncing the culprit! Here Fluffy had dwelt as long as he could remember anything.

All he knew was that he was not born in the Buildings, and that his father had not taken to drink and evil ways when "mother" married him; but as she always began to cry if he asked her about her earlier days, Fluffy got to understand that there was something about them which was not to be spoken of.

It had only been for a year or so that Fluffy had taken to sell papers or matches to try and help get a living. Until that time his mother had worked at a laundry, while he played in the court, for this was before the days of school-boards and fines.

They had not been so very poor then—miserably dirty and ill-clad of course, but that was not unusual in Dockett's-buildings. By poor, Fluffy understood going hungry day after day, and nothing in the room left to pawn. When mother's earnings at the laundry brought enough to eat and drink, he did not feel badly off, although his knees and elbows could be seen through the rents of his clothes, and his boots were safely "put away" at the neighbouring pawnbroker's until required for some special occasion.

Living with his so-called "granny" his

meals were uncertain, both as to time and quantity. There were days when *she* required nothing but what she sent the little boy to fetch from the public-house; days in which she was apt to be first quarrelsome, then low-spirited, and finally oblivious of Fluffy and everything else in heavy drunken sleep. At such times he was more than usually clamorous with his *Echoes* or fusees, and hung about bakers' doors or the tempting windows of the cookshops, hoping that some one might take pity on him and give him a treat.

There were, however, times when Granny made great and good resolutions, when she even went the length of a little sweeping and cleaning, and talked of taking the pledge —these were red-letter days in Fluffy's calendar, days when there was almost unlimited bread and butter, with some savoury

2

addition in the shape of bloaters or a rasher of bacon. Nay, he had even been seen bearing a joint upon a layer of potatoes to the baker's round the corner, while Granny watched at the door, broom in hand, ready to run out and inflict punishment upon any urchin who should seriously impede his passage through the court.

Never having been to school, it is not to be wondered at if Fluffy could neither read nor write proficiently ; I say *proficiently*, because in some unknown way he had gained as much knowledge as enabled him to spell out some of the verses in penny song-books, and to get an idea of what the *Police News* contained. He had even learned enough writing to manage some remarks in chalk upon the neighbours' doors, when so inclined, always taking care not to be seen doing it. Thus had our poor little

Fluffy passed through eleven years of his life, and he never looked forward to anything very different. But though his mind rarely turned to the future at all, it often travelled back in a wondering, puzzled way to his mother's death. In his own fashion he had loved her, for she had not often beaten or ill-used him, as many of the boys' mothers did, and when she had grown weak and ill, and was forced to leave off her laundry work altogether, Fluffy began to try and earn something, so that she might not starve. It would have come very near to it, only the neighbours were kind, as the poor mostly are when one of their own class is really suffering. Even the hard old landlady let the rent run on, and said nothing very strong, though sometimes she would mutter to the effect that "when folks *must* die, it was hard for 'em to be so long about

2—2

it, keeping a poor widder from letting her room, and not paying a farthing of rent neither."

But though long and painful, the end came at last, and Fluffy found himself crying over mother—a white, still mother, who would never look, never speak to him more.

When he saw the coffin lowered into the pauper's grave, Fluffy had all manner of strange thoughts about it, thoughts which came back afterwards many and many a night as he stood in the cold, wet street, plying his small trade, or trudging wearily home to Granny, and the noise and dirt of Dockett's-buildings.

He had heard his mother say many a time when things were hard, that she should have no rest till she was in her grave; when she died, some of the women, thinking to comfort the lonely boy, had told him she was "better

off," and yet Fluffy could not help a shudder
as the earth was shovelled in upon the coffin,
and he came away with the sense of being
quite solitary and uncared-for in this great
busy world.

If that was the end of all, if *that* was
being "better off," the child felt as if he
would rather live on in all the misery and
want which surrounded him; and he could
not think of the grave-yard, and his mother
lying there, without a sense of fear that increased as weeks passed on.

On the cheerless night when we have seen
Fluffy conversing with his former neighbour,
he felt unusually tired and spiritless. It
may be that rough Joe's contempt for him
and his efforts to earn money had damped
his courage, for Fluffy even forgot his dread
of the pauper's coffin and grave, so far as to
" wish he was dead." He did not mean it

though, for as he wended his way through narrow streets and turnings, which were so many " short cuts" home, his thoughts had taken quite a different shape, and were wholly given to the consideration of whether supper would be forthcoming or not.

Granny had been drinking hard for several days ; it was about time for one of her fits of passing contrition and better purpose, so with this hope breaking in upon his own dejection, Fluffy's slow walk became a brisk trot, until his journey ended, and the noise of angry voices proclaimed that he was just arriving at Dockett's-buildings—just " home."

## CHAPTER II.

THE disturbance which Fluffy heard before he turned into the court proved to be nothing more uncommon than a quarrel between some of the occupants of the house in which he dwelt. Stopping on the edge of the crowd which had collected, he gained the intelligence that the "first-floor front" and the "third-floor back" had fallen out, and were settling the difference with threats and abusive words, which bade fair to end in blows unless some policeman interfered.

It was, however, supposed that the police did not care to penetrate too closely or too frequently into the doings of the inhabitants of Dockett's-buildings, for it was but rarely that they interfered in the brawling and rioting which went on there.

It was an understood thing, it seemed, that the court was a den of misery and degradation, and no one could make it better, therefore no one tried. The families who lived there were constantly changing. Taking their rooms by the week they left them at a short notice—sometimes without notice at all, and in the darkness of night if there was rent owing which it was inconvenient to pay. The only person who seemed stationary was old Mrs. Ward, "Granny Ward" as she was called by all her neighbours, and therefore by Fluffy also, whom she had in a sort of fashion adopted when his mother died.

She was always talking of turning him adrift though, complaining that she was too

poor to keep other folks' children. Sometimes Fluffy thought he should not be much
worse off if she did; nay, viewed in the
distance, there was something exciting in
the idea of being "on his own hook," as
he expressed it.

On this particular night when he hoped
there would be some supper forthcoming,
Granny was very desponding — into the
workhouse she must go ; and as for any
thing to eat, there was bread, and if that
would not do he might earn for himself.

Poor Fluffy looked at his waste *Echoes*,
feeling that it was not for want of trying
that he was not independent; but he said
nothing as he took the bread she offered
him, only began to think more seriously of
running off altogether from Granny and
Dockett's-buildings. As for her going into .
the workhouse, Fluffy did not in the least

believe it. If all the folks said she'd got
money laid by somewhere though she *did*
live in the damp kitchen, there must be truth
in it; besides was not it her house, and was
not she sharper in looking after her rent than
any other of the owners of the tumble-down
dilapidated dwellings ? Clearly Granny's
extreme poverty was a pretence, and Fluffy
felt very much aggrieved at the lack of
bloaters or other savoury dish, and wished
ever so much that Joe Rogers had taken
him into his own line of business.

It was late when the boy laid himself
down on the mattress in the corner, and
later still when he fell asleep to dream that
he was feasting on saveloys with Joe.

It was fine and bright when Fluffy got to
the City with his papers next morning, but
his dirty face looked almost more forlorn
in the sunshine than it had done under the

flaring gas-lights, and Rogers coming by again, laughed more than ever at his appearance.

" I'm most inclined to take you along of me," he said, eying Fluffy from top to toe. " You might make yourself useful, though for the matter of that I know lots of chaps as'd do better."

" Oh, do take me, Joe," said Fluffy. " I'd give anything to get clear of Granny."

" You'll keep away from her and the whole lot of them then ?" inquired Joe. " You'll shut your mouth about what I'm doing if I take you, eh ?"

Fluffy promised that he would.

" Well then, come along. I always was a good-natured chap, wasn't I ?" said Joe; and Fluffy said " Yes," although he had only known his acquaintance as the most quarrelsome bully and coward of all whom he had ever come across.

They walked on together through the busy streets quietly enough for some time, and Fluffy almost wondered at Joe's sedate expression and manner, and especially at the politeness with which he apologised to any elderly gentleman whom he might accidentally jostle on the crowded footway.

But after a while they left the thoroughfares and turned into less respectable parts of London, where Joe's spirits began to rise and his manner to resume its usual style. He was evidently well-satisfied about something he had accomplished, and made allusions to the special luck which had befallen him that morning. All this puzzled Fluffy, but he asked no questions, and tried to laugh as loudly and as often as his friend. He took a share of some beer which Joe called for at a low public-house where he seemed well known, and came out feeling rather unsteady on his legs though more excited in his spirits than when he entered. Fluffy was not unused to such refreshment, but then he had only partaken of the small quantities he could sip between the public-house at the corner of Dockett's-buildings and Granny Ward's door; now—fasting from the night before —what Joe had given him was almost more than he could manage.

"I've got some very pertickler bisness as I must do by myself now," said his friend. "You wait here, Fluffy, till I come back. I'll not be five minutes."

Fluffy could not refuse, but he half-suspected some trick, and looked dejectedly after Joe as he darted round a corner and was lost to sight. But true to his word he came back, and with wonderful generosity gave a sixpence to Fluffy. "I'll make you a present of it," he said, with a patronising air. "You can't be expected to learn my trade the first day."

"Are you going to any work, Joe?" Fluffy ventured to ask as he pocketed the sixpence.

The elder boy's face wore a curious expression, and he gave a low whistle before he replied.

"Mine's not what you may call a common bisness," he said at last. "It don't go on at no shop, nor it don't want no governor. As for customers, I knows where to find 'em."

Fluffy's puzzled face was a delight to Joe, and he broke into a loud laugh.

"Look 'ere, my young innercent," he said when he had somewhat recovered himself; "I've been doin' bisness while we've been

walkin' along so quiet and so comfortable.
You'd never have thought that, would you
now ?"

Fluffy owned that he never should.

" You didn't notice how pertickler fond I
were of the respectable streets where there's
such a lot of fine swells a-goin' to their
horffices and places ?"

" Yes, I did think of that," said Fluffy,
still in the dark as to the nature of Joe's
calling.

" The old uns is the best," said the lad,
with a chuckle. " And if you wants to
know for why, it's because they carries the
real good old silk 'andkerchiefs as gen'le-
men ought, not your common white rags as
fetches next to nothing."

A sudden light broke upon Fluffy's un-
derstanding.

"You never mean as you've been pickin'

pockets, and me never so much as guessin'? You *are* a clever 'un, Joe."

His face beamed with approval of his friend's wit and ability; such an idea had never come into his head when *he* was wondering how to get a living, but then he was not as sharp and knowing as Joe.

Only a very slight consciousness of sin connected with such a course occurred to this untaught boy, but the risk of being found out was clear to him, and he wondered how his friend managed.

"Don't you never get into trouble about it?" he asked. "Don't you never have the perlice after you?"

Joe laughed. "I've give 'em the slip up to now, though I won't say I've not come near being caught. I'd get over it if I was, bless you, and at it again as soon as convenient; it's a capital way of livin',

Fluffy—ever so much better than tryin' to sell *Echoes*, I can tell you."

Fluffy agreed, and paid marked attention while Joe " put him up to the dodge," as he expressed it ; and at the close of the day he was proud to show one article as the result of his first lesson in stealing.

When night had quite closed in and the London streets grew deserted by the more respectable class of people, Joe led the way to a public-house, where he obtained some beer and eatables for himself and Fluffy.

" Ain't mine a good line of trade?" he asked as they despatched their supper. "Ain't this better than a-tryin' to sell *Echoes* and a-livin' on what old Granny Ward 'll give you ?"

" I should think it were," responded Fluffy, with his mouth full. " Do you allers have as good a day as this, Joe ?"

" Well, no," said the elder boy, reflecting. "No, I can't rightly say I do. Some days the old gents is that perwerse and sharp there's no doin' anything. Sometimes it's the bobbies as persists in keeping their eye on yer. Still, one day with another, I gets on tolerably well; mostly has enough to eat and all that."

" Where d'ye live, Joe ?" said Fluffy, when their meal was drawing to a close.

" Live! why anywhere or nowhere, whichever yer likes to call it," said Joe. " I gets my wittles anywhere as is convenient, and I sleeps at any lodging as turns up handy when it's night and bisness is over."

Fluffy said nothing, but as he followed his companion out into the street he wondered whether he was to accompany him to the place he might choose to shelter in that night, or whether, on the strength of the sixpence he had received, he was to provide for himself.

Hardly were they outside, however, before Joe cleared up the difficulty. " I think I've done 'andsome by yer," he said, clapping Fluffy roughly on the back. " I've shown yer 'ow to do bisness, and I've give yer sixpence, and I've stood the beer and wittles, and yer do get through them surprisin' for one of your size. And what 'ave yer done for all this ? Why, only just took one 'andkerchief and that a white un. You won't pay for your keep at that rate."

Fluffy hung his head. " Yer might think as it's the first day, and I'm new to it all, Joe. I'll do more to-morrow I dare say."

" It's to be 'oped so," responded Joe.

" You makes precious sure I'm a-goin' to keep you on, don't you ? However I don't mind another day ; you're only a beginner, and there's not much to be expected of yer. Come along, and I'll stand the lodgin';" and so saying Joe turned into a dark unlighted alley which seemed familiar to him, and stumbling his way after, Fluffy found himself in a sort of cellar already crowded with the very lowest and vilest occupants. Even *he* had never before set foot in a den like this.

# CHAPTER III.

"Has anybody seen that there good-for-nothin' boy?" said old Granny Ward, as she stood in her doorway, accosting all who passed in and out of Dockett's-buildings the first night of Fluffy's absence. But no one had seen or heard of him, and only one or two idle women even cared to listen to the news of his disappearance.

All day long Granny had not noticed his absence, for it was a common thing for him to keep clear of her till late in the evening, but now it was just twelve o'clock, and there was no sign of his coming, and at last the old woman put out her candle and laid herself down to sleep, muttering threats of how she would "pay" Fluffy when he *did* arrive.

But when another day and night had passed, and nothing was known of the boy, Granny Ward grew very uneasy. It was not because of any love she bore him, for all the softer, kinder parts of her nature had perished long before. She had kept Fluffy only with the thought of having some one to "do" for her as she got older, and now to lose him when he was just getting of an age to be useful, was most annoying to her.

"Audacious, ungrateful little rascal," she said, when her neighbours asked if there was any tidings of Fluffy, "I'll make him remember this when he does come back. I'll teach him not to go a-running away from me again."

It never seemed possible that Fluffy should have departed altogether, and she

believed it was only a question of waiting a
week at most, and he would turn up a trifle
dirtier and more ragged, perhaps, than when
she last saw him. Still it annoyed her to
be asked about the boy, and discovering this,
it was the favourite amusement of the urchins
of Dockett's-buildings to put their heads in
at the door and shout, "I say, where's Fluffy?"
to escape again with a shrill whistle, as the
old woman vainly tried to catch the offender.

Many polite inquiries of the same nature
were chalked upon her door late at night or
in early morning, when it happened to be
closed, and altogether Fluffy's name was a
great discomfort to Granny Ward just then.

A week went by, and stretched into
another, and still the runaway did not appear. It was just three weeks after his
departure that a dirty lad who lived on the
opposite side of the court, called out of the

top window to Granny Ward as she went her way to the public-house :

"I say, I knows where Fluffy is."

Now Mrs. Ward was not unused to such information, and was therefore inclined to be hard of belief. Scarcely a boy or girl either, but told wild tales of having seen Fluffy—sometimes "all dressed up like a genel'man," at others " a reg'lar smart footman, and no mistake," but always happy and prosperous.

It was not therefore surprising that upon the present occasion the old woman passed on without heeding, as her name echoed through the court, nor did she take any further notice on her return than to shake her fist at the opposite house, and scream some threat which was lost in the shouts of the children who were playing at hop-scotch on the footway.

"I say, Granny," persisted the boy, thrusting his rough mop of a head farther out, and raising his voice, "I ain't a-gammonin' yer. I knows where Fluffy is, and no mistake; me and Bill saw a fellow as told us last night——"

Still Granny Ward affected not to care, and the boy's voice rose higher and higher, until all the court came out to listen.

"Fluffy's been took up, he has. He's got three months, and no mistake."

The old woman emerged from her kitchen at that.

"Took up, has he?" she cried. "Serve him right, too. You come down and tell me all about it, and I'll give you a penny."

"Show us the penny first," said the boy, and there was a general laugh, as Granny fumbled in her pocket for the coin.

"Jist you 'old it up and let's see it's a

real genewine copper," continued her opposite
neighbour; and then as Granny obeyed, he
requested one of his friends below to bring
it up to him.

"I said as you'd got to come down here,"
objected Mrs. Ward.

"And I ain't a-goin' to," was the rejoinder.
"Jest as yer please. Keep yer penny, and I'll
keep my news, or hand it over to Charlie
Simmonds there, as'll bring it up to me."

After some grumbling the transaction was
concluded, and Master Bob Harvey told his
story from the top window to an admiring
audience of men, women, and boys.

The general feeling was one of admiration
not unmixed with surprise, for Fluffy had
been thought little of in the court, and now
more than one voice was heard to declare
that "they shouldn't have thought he'd the
pluck for it."

To be in prison was something of a distinction in those parts rather than a disgrace.
It must have taken a certain amount of
daring and defiance of law to get there at
all, and Dockett's-buildings was antagonistic
to law in any shape.

To know then that Fluffy was in prison,
and for pocket-picking too, was quite an interesting thing ; the one regret being that
none of his old friends were present at the
trial, to show by that means their sympathy
and approval.

Though Granny Ward affected to believe
that he would "come to the gallows," she
was inwardly proud of him, and did not fail
to inquire of the company she met upon her
next visit to the public-house, whether they
had heard that "Fluffy'd been took up."

Meanwhile Fluffy himself was far from
elated.  He had enjoyed his wild life with

Joe and Joe's companions—it was so new a thing to have plenty to eat and a few pence in his pocket, that he willingly put up with a little rough usage. He had thought now and then during those three weeks at his "trade" that it was a risky way of living, one which might end in a visit to a police-court any day, but the very excitement of the thing had a charm, and if Joe baffled the police, why also should not he?

But now all was over, for three months at least, and Fluffy would almost have regretted leaving Granny Ward and Dockett's-buildings, if he had not been better off for food even in prison than in the old days.

The order and silence alone were almost unbearable to the wild little fellow, who had been free to run hither and thither as he willed, ever since he could remember anything.

As often happens in such cases, Joe, the oldest and chief offender, had escaped, while Fluffy—being less expert—was caught in the very act of picking an old gentleman's pocket in Cheapside, and handed over to a police-constable.

No shame, no sorrow, were in the boy's heart. How should there be when he knew nothing of God or God's laws? He knew of course that the people among whom he had passed his life, not unfrequently got lodged in prison for various offences, and for varying periods of confinement; but all he felt was a rebellious hatred of those who enforced order, and a longing desire to be out again, in the company of Joe Rogers.

The first time that a thorough conscious-ness of sin dawned upon Fluffy's mind, was on the first Sunday when he attended the prison service, and heard the chaplain preach.

He never meant to listen—he was busy thinking of his former companions, and trying to imagine what crowded church Joe would pass into in hope of finding a chance to steal, when all at once he heard a word which roused his attention, and after that he could not form any pictures of Joe's doings : "God saw you." Fluffy did not know what had been said before, but he heard that, and felt cold and frightened when the preacher added, "God sees you now, and not only sees you outwardly, but into every dark corner of your heart—yes, even into the very sins which perhaps you are thinking of doing in the future."

Though he did not half understand what was meant, it was a most uncomfortable thought to Fluffy that *any one* should see into his thoughts like that; and although he wanted not to believe it, he could not quite free himself from the uneasiness such words caused him.

But when he heard more—heard that even while He saw the black stains of sin upon his soul, even though He had seen every hidden sin of his life, this God loved him, Fluffy wondered very much. In simple words the chaplain told of the proof of this great, wonderful love ; how God had made Himself man in the person of Jesus Christ, and come down to earth to live, and then to die for sinners. As he listened to this strange new story—new to his ears, though so sweet and so old a story to most of us—he forgot all about Joe Rogers, and even ceased to remember the terrible fact that there was an All-seeing God ; nay, as he heard of the cruel sufferings of Jesus, of His agony, His thirst, His nailing to the cross, Fluffy's head sunk lower and lower, until it was bowed upon his breast, and tears started into the eyes which had never yet wept for his sins or for the sufferings of others.　In after days, he would wonder whether there had been more said that day —whether the chaplain had told of the return Christ asks for all He suffered to redeem men ; but then, one thought, and only one, could sink down into his innermost heart— that for *him*, poor little guilty prisoner as he was, some one had died upon the Cross, some one who loved him more than he could understand.

## CHAPTER IV.

SLOWLY, but surely, Fluffy's three months'
punishment passed by. He had earned
a very good character in the prison, and the
chaplain had stood his friend. He would
talk to the boy now and then, listening with
a great pity to the story of his life, a common one, alas! to his ears. He would
speak to Fluffy of God and His commandments, and the punishment which follows
sin, both in this world and the next, and
tell him too of Christ Who died upon the
Cross that sinners might be saved. It was
like a wonderful story to this ignorant little
fellow, and one which always moistened his

4

eyes with tears, and yet he could not very clearly understand how all this suffering was to benefit him and make him better.

" You must believe Christ died to save you," the chaplain would say when Fluffy tried to explain his doubtful misgivings; yet his words seemed to fall short of what was necessary, and if he could but have put something more practical before the boy the difficulty would have been cleared up. But Mr. Morton could not do this. His heart was full of compassion for the sinful people with whom he had to do. He could draw tears from their eyes many a Sunday when in the prison pulpit he told of Christ's love to each one of them, of Christ's voice calling every one of them to come and lay down their sins at His feet, and be healed and forgiven. All this he told, all this he did faithfully and earnestly, according to the

light he had. If he had but known the true
Faith, the complete Faith of Christ's Church,
he could have told these poor sinners not of
God's grace alone, but of the means of ob-
taining it—of those sacraments which convey
peace and healing to the soul.

So the day came when Fluffy was free.
He had not been able to sleep all night for
thinking of it, wondering where he should
go and what should become of him when
those heavy prison gates should unclose and
let him out into the London streets once
more.

Should he go to Dockett's-buildings?
Fluffy thought not. No sense of shame held
him back, for he knew his old acquaintances
sufficiently well to know also that he would
figure somewhat highly in the court now,
and that boys who had once despised would
now condescend to " chum" with him be-

cause he had earned the distinction of im-
prisonment.

But Fluffy had tasted the sweets of
liberty—liberty from Granny Ward's au-
thority, and even if it was accompanied by
many a hardship he had a mind to be independent of her once more.   Not to take up
with Joe Rogers, though—he promised Mr.
Morton that, when the chaplain bade the lad
good-bye and put a half-crown into his hand.

" Keep honest, whatever you do," he had
said ; and Fluffy answered " Yes, sir," without hesitation, although he partly understood that it would be a difficult matter.

His hands trembled with eagerness as he
put on the ragged clothing which he had
worn when he was taken up.   The three
long months were over now, and Fluffy
realised that he was once more himself and
not a prisoner.

Not quite the same as he had been, though. As the great gate swung back to let him through, Fluffy thought of what he had learned there; that God had seen every day and hour of his life—those sinful days and hours ; nay more, that He would see him now, go where he would, and see all that he did, and all that was done by his chosen companions. It brought uneasiness to Fluffy's mind which nothing he had learned seemed to dispel.

"He said I'd only got to b'lieve, Mr. Morton did," he muttered to himself, as he glanced back at the gloomy prison walls. "In course I b'lieves all he said about the Lord Jesus Christ. I don't suppose as a gentleman like him, as give me a half-crown too, would tell me lies. I b'lieves every bit on it, and that He died on a Cross for me; but it don't seem to make me no better, not one bit," and Fluffy's face grew very downcast.

He was roused by a cheerful salutation, proceeding from none other than his former friend Joe, who now clapped him on the back with an energy that was not altogether pleasant.

"Hallo, young un," he cried, "I know'd as your time was up, so I came to meet you. I'm a fellow as is always ready to stand by a friend. Cheer up, Fluffy! never say die! you and me 'll get along better than ever."

"Let me alone, do," said Fluffy, still minding his promise to Mr. Morton.

"What, you ain't a-goin' to turn sulky, are you?" said Joe. "I won't have you along of me if you cuts up rough like that."

"I'm not a-goin' along of you," said Fluffy. "I'm a-goin' to work and keep myself honest;" and to this he kept, though Joe tried the influence of ridicule, persuasion, and abuse.

"Well, I'll give you something as a keep-sake afore we part," said the cowardly lad, striking Fluffy several times about the head, so violently, that at last he fell. Joe was off then, for a woman who came by showed an inclination to collar and shake *him* in her sympathy for Fluffy, and a crowd collecting was not what Joe desired.

"What have you been a-doin' of ?" said the new comer, picking up Fluffy's cap, and brushing some of the dust and dirt from him as he got up from the pavement where Joe had thrown him.

"Nothing," said Fluffy, half sullen, half crying.

"You've been a-fighting or something ; I know you have," continued the woman. "All the same he's a big coward, whoever he is, for knocking down a little chap like you. There, go home to your mother, do," and away she went, leaving Fluffy to gaze after her with a despondent face, and a still more sorrowful heart.

Somehow he felt as if he should like to have told her he had no home, and no mother to go to. She had a kind face, though her words were rough, and perhaps she could have told him where he might find a lodging. With half-a-crown in his possession Fluffy felt quite rich enough to think of a lodging. To him it was a very mine of wealth, and he could scarcely realise the uncertainty of his future prospects with this bright new half-crown in the pocket of his tattered corduroys. Oh, if Joe Rogers had known of his riches ! Fluffy's eyes brightened at the thought of what his vexation would be, could he but find out that he—the clever picker of gentlemen's pockets—had failed to secure the treasure hidden in corduroy.

Almost without knowing where his feet were carrying him, Fluffy sauntered through the streets, always keeping a sharp look-out lest he might encounter Joe Rogers.

It was not, however, very probable ; Joe's line of employment kept him busy in the better parts of the town, while Fluffy, from habit and old acquaintance, preferred the narrower streets and alleys, in which other boys walked, whose trousers also were jagged about the ankles, and whose boots were scarcely worth the name.

After a long time he found himself in the neighbourhood of Holborn—a narrow turning in which there were several small shops, one of which, a broker's, displayed such a variety of household goods that Fluffy was quite attracted.

A sudden idea came to him as he gazed.
Why should he not get a place at some such
shop ? A sharp boy who could keep his eye
upon the goods, and answer the inquiries of
customers must surely be useful, and no one
answering to that description appeared to
be within. Only a woman could Fluffy discern standing back in the shop, with a baby
in her arms, and another little child clinging
to her skirt.

The lads of Dockett's-buildings are not
as a rule hindered by shyness from making
their desires known, neither was Fluffy.

Stepping just within the doorway, he
made his inquiry, and took a glance at his
reflection in an old mirror at one and the
same moment.

No ; she wanted no boy, so the woman
said, nor did Fluffy's persuasions move her.
At last he gave it up as a bad job, and was

turning away from the shop when his way was stopped by a lad not much older evidently than himself, who was examining a small hanging book-case with great interest.

Fluffy stood by and listened to the bargaining which followed, and finally saw the purchase effected and the price paid.

" You'll find it rather a job to carry it all the way home," said the mistress of the shop, who seemed to have some acquaintance with her customer.

The boy laughed merrily. " *That* a job to carry, that bit of a thing! Why I'd carry two of 'em, and not mind it, Mrs. Parker."

" All the same you might let that poor chap there take it for you," said the woman, pointing to Fluffy. "He was in here bothering about a place just now, and I dare say he'd be glad of a job."

But still the lad laughed. " No, thank

you, Mrs. Parker, I'm not a grand swell who wants an errand-boy. I'll take it and glad; it's just the thing I've been looking for this long time."

He was about to shoulder it and go his way, when Fluffy darted forward: "I'll carry it for you, master. I'll take it for three-pence anywhere, and tuppence if 'tain't fur."

"No, thank you," was the reply; but then the boy glanced at Fluffy, taking in his sharp face and tattered garments, and with a quick instinct he said, "All right. Pick it up and come along, though I don't want you to come all the way. Mother *would* laugh if I couldn't manage that bit of a book-shelf myself."

So off they started, Fluffy a pace or two behind the tidily-dressed boy, whom he eyed with a mixture of admiration and curiosity.

For about five minutes they walked along in silence, during which Fluffy found out that this other boy had a bright pleasant face, and in his neat clothing seemed almost a gentleman to *him*, the ragged, well-nigh barefoot urchin just out of jail.

"Well, what are you thinking of ?" he said presently, slackening his pace, and turning a pair of bright dark eyes full upon his rather disreputable companion.

"Thinkin' of you," was Fluffy's reply—a reply which brought a short merry laugh from the other lad.

"Well, and what about me ?" he asked, still keeping by Fluffy's side.

"I was a-wonderin' who you are, and where you comes from."

"I'll tell you. My name is Murphy— Charlie Murphy, and I live at Westminster,

I don't suppose you're much the wiser now, are you?"

"I know Westminster pretty well," returned Fluffy. "I s'pose you're Irish, seein' your name's Murphy."

"Well, not exactly. That is, I've never been in Ireland, no more's father, but we're come of an Irish family."

"I thought as much," said Fluffy, and then they walked on a minute or so in silence.

"Why don't you tell me what's *your* name and where *you* were from now?" said Charlie Murphy.

"'Cause you didn't ask me," said Fluffy.

"Well, I'm asking you now. Who are you, and where do you live?"

"Don't live nowheres partikler. Used to live in Dockett's-buildings, but moved three months ago," said Fluffy, trying to be amusing.

"And where have you been since?" asked Murphy.

"Ah, that's tellin'. I've been a-visitin', that's where I've been."

The other lad scanned Fluffy from head to foot with a somewhat doubtful air. "Well, tell me what's your name then?"

"Fluffy," was the reply, with such a grin upon the dirty face that Charlie believed he was joking.

"Come now, don't be a young fool," he said. "I told you my name and you've got to tell me yours."

"I've told you," said Fluffy. "I've not got no long name like big swells such as you, 'tain't likely."

"I'm not a swell," said Charlie hotly. "You know that fast enough. Father's only a workman, but he's one of the best in his trade, and I don't want to be thought any different to what I am."

"You needn't get so riled about it," said Fluffy coolly. "I didn't know nothin' about you nor your father either, and you're somethin' like a swell alongside of me."

Again Charlie Murphy looked him down from head to foot. "They haven't taken much care of your clothes certainly where you've been," he remarked. "What did you call yourself ?"

"Fluffy," was the reply. "If you go on a arskin' of me from now till to-morrow I can't tell you no different. I allers was told as I were Fluffy, and nothin' else."

"You couldn't ever have been given such a name," said the other lad. "It's some nickname I suppose. Why don't you ask your mother your right name ?"

" Ain't got no mother," said Fluffy;
" she died awhile back."

" Well, your father then ?"

" Ain't got no father ; he'd cut off some-
wheres long afore mother died."

" Well then, your grandmother, or whoever looks after you ?" persisted Charlie.

Fluffy laughed. " Bless yer heart, master,
there's no one looks after me exceptin' the
perlice, as is more attentive than one could
wish. I takes care of myself."

" And very bad care too, I should say,"
remarked the other lad gravely. " Did you
ever go to school or learn anything ?"

Fluffy shook his head, and proceeded to
whistle some favourite street air as a proof
of his indifference to everything, and once
more there was silence till they reached the
corner of the next street.

" Here's threepence, and you needn't

**5**

come any farther. Good-bye, Fluffy," and away went Charlie Murphy with his purchase under his arm, while the street boy gazed after him with a regretful kind of look in his eyes.

" He *is* a nice-lookin' chap, and no mistake. I'd like to change places with him, that I should," said Fluffy, leaning wearily against the lamp-post, as he wondered what to be doing now.

He had bought a couple of sausage-rolls at a cook-shop some time before he met young Murphy, so he was not yet hungry ; he had still a good part of the half-crown left and his newly-earned threepence, so that he did not feel poor. It was the great sense of loneliness which came over him and brought the shadow to his face ; and in that loneliness he could almost have wished himself once more in the company of Joe Rogers, or old Granny Ward.

# CHAPTER V.

A NEAT comfortable-looking woman stood in
the doorway of one of the houses of a quiet
street in the district of Westminster, which
was Charlie Murphy's home. Her voice too
sounded pleasant and cheery as she welcomed
the boy and admired his purchase; hearing
with interest how much was asked, how
much he gave, and what a capital bargain
had been made.

"I got it in Holborn, but I didn't carry
it all the way myself, mother," said Charlie,
as he stood hammer in hand to fix up the
shelf in a space which seemed left on purpose
for it upon the wall.

" Not carry it yourself ! Why you're not fancying yourself weak, Charlie !" laughed Mrs. Murphy as she looked proudly at the lad's strong well-built figure and healthy cheeks.

" I thought you'd say something like that, mother," said Charlie. " No, I'd have carried that and two or three more, only there was a poor wretched little chap wanted to earn a few coppers, and I let him come the best part of the way. He'd been in at Parker's asking if they'd take him as a shop-boy."

" Ah ! there's more boys after places than places that want boys," said Mrs. Murphy, bustling about to get dinner ready, while Charlie arranged his books, retreating a pace or two every now and again to observe the effect.

" There now, I think that's nice," he said,

when he had finished his task to his satisfaction. "I tell you what, mother, I'm hungry. This cold day makes a fellow sharp."

"And here's father," said Mrs. Murphy, looking out of the window, and then hurrying to the door, just as she had hurried to meet Charlie.

Before five minutes were over, father, mother, and son were seated at their dinner. A pleasant, happy-faced group to look upon. Once it had been larger, but Charley now was the only child remaining to them ; and as for him, his mother declared "you wouldn't find a better boy or one more regular at his duties if you looked London through."

Come of a good old Irish family, both Patrick Murphy and his wife had kept their Faith burning brightly in their hearts, and

Charley took after them, as boys mostly do after good Christian parents. He was a merry, light-hearted fellow too; no one more fond of frolic and mischief, and therefore a favourite with other boys. But it was an understood thing among them that it would not do to say aught against Charley's Faith, or to do what that Faith taught him was wrong—to offend in either of these two points was to rouse the Irish blood in his veins.

Just now, as he despatched his dinner with a boy's hearty appetite, he could not help thinking of Fluffy.

"I wish that poor little chap I saw this morning had some of this to keep the cold out," he said, and then he told all he knew of the boy whom he had met with outside the broker's shop.

"It's a dreadful thing—dreadful!" said

Mrs. Murphy. "No mother nor father, nor home either : and there are hundreds and thousands as bad off. Dear, dear ! I'd like to be a great lady, and put them all into good Catholic schools, that I would," she added.

"I'm thinking we working folks are too much given to trusting that sort of thing to great folks," said Murphy, laying down his knife and fork. "If we were to do our part, there'd not be so much misery and sin in the world, maybe."

Mrs. Murphy looked puzzled.

"I don't know, I'm sure, what we could do. You're in good work, thank God; still, we've got to live and pay our way, and I don't see how we can afford to give more than we do already to things."

"It wasn't giving in the way of money I was thinking of," said Murphy. "It only

came into my mind that even Charlie here
could be some good to one of these poor
little chaps like he's been telling of. He
could give him a few cast-off things now
and then, and a bit to eat, that we should
never miss; aye, and a kind word that
don't cost anything, and which would
make way for a word about God and His
Blessed Mother. I may be wrong, or I may
be right," said Murphy, "rising from the
table to say grace; "but that's what often
comes into my mind;" and away he went to
his work, leaving Charlie and his mother to
talk it over.

"There's a deal of truth in what father
says," exclaimed Mrs. Murphy as the door
closed. "There's not a better man, nor one
with more sense living than your father,
Charlie."

The boy laughed. Although he quite

agreed in his mother's opinion, he often did laugh at her declaration that no woman ever had a husband or son to equal hers.

"Yes, I dare say," he said; "but it's all very well for father to pitch it all on to me. I'd like to know how I'm to talk to a little chap and do him any good. I shouldn't know what to say."

"More shame to you then," replied his mother. "Brought up as you've been, and learned your catechism through and through, and Father Dunstan taking such pains as he does with all you boys."

"Don't go on at a fellow like that, mother," said Charlie. "I meant that I didn't quite like to go preaching to other chaps; it don't seem in my way, you see."

"Father didn't say anything about preaching," said Mrs. Murphy. "It was about helping some poor boy and saying a kind word to him that *he* was talking of ;" and then she went into the little back kitchen to wash up plates and dishes, leaving Charlie to his own reflections.

It was still holiday-time. Christmas and New Year had but just passed, and there was a week now before school re-opened. But time never hung heavily on Charlie Murphy's hands. It had been fine frosty weather—just the weather for sliding and skating in the park ; and then at home he had his books to read, to say nothing of sundry jobs of carpentering which always seemed wanting by his mother. Yet now, he stood with his hands in his pockets looking out of the window as if he had hardly made up his mind what to do—nor had he. He seemed to see a picture rise up before him of Fluffy, ragged, dirty, homeless—a boy not much younger than himself, but oh !

how differently circumstanced. And, then
Charlie's head began to puzzle over a subject
which many older and wiser heads have pon-
dered—how was it that there was this strange
inequality in life ? why did God ordain that
some should be born in misery and ignor-
ance and sin, while others were surrounded
by comfort, blessing, and grace from their
earliest infancy ?

"I can't make it out," said Charlie to
himself, and a sort of conviction came into
his mind that it was one of those things we
never can "make out," but which we know
are part of God's good Providence. A conviction too, that it might be God's purpose
to keep the sight of poverty and suffering—
yes, and sin—always before us that we may
relieve the sorrow, pity the sin, in remembrance of Him Who took upon Himself a life
of poverty and "had not where to lay His

head," that He might take away, by His own
suffering, the sin which separates mankind
from God.

I do not tell you that Charlie Murphy
realised all this, but some vague feeling of it
was in his heart, and something seemed to
keep before him the picture of poor tattered
Fluffy, and whispered, "Inasmuch as ye have
done it unto one of these, my least brethren,
you have done it unto me."

"Mother, I'm going out a bit," he said,
turning into the little back kitchen ; "I'm
going back to where I left that little chap
this morning. It isn't more than two hours
ago, and perhaps he's hanging about somewhere. I might find out where he *does*
live."

"Ah, do," said Mrs. Murphy. "And
Charlie, if he'd come along with you as far
as this, I'd have a good thick slice of bread

and butter for him, and that old jacket of yours that you've grown out of. I dare say he is not so broad as you."

"All right, mother," and away went Charley—to meet his friend Denis Smith at the very door.

"Just the chap I wanted," he cried. "Come for a walk, Charlie."

"Oh, it's no use," said Charlie, wishing to find an excuse; "the ice won't bear now."

"I know that, but it's no use stopping in. Holidays won't last much longer, so come along."

"I'm going somewhere particular," said Charlie.

"Oh, bother! let it wait and come along with me."

Charlie hesitated. Denis Smith was his great friend—a good friend too, who never led him into any harm, though now he was unconsciously tempting him from his duty.

With a boy's weakness, Charlie did not like to persist in refusing the company of Denis—after all it would be just as easy to seek out Fluffy to-morrow, he was not *obliged* to do it that very day.

With these excuses in answer to the up-braiding of conscience, Charlie went off with Denis ; but never before had an afternoon seemed so dull, and never before had he been such a spiritless companion.

" What's the matter, old fellow ?" said Denis again and again ; but he only got one answer, and that was " Nothing."

" *Nothing !*" that meant a vision of a small figure in ragged clothing, so ragged that you could see his shoulders through the rents in his jacket ; a face with a sharp, shrewd expression on it, which told a tale of

familiarity with vice and crime, and yet in
spite of all it was a weary, lonely little face,
which would have stirred any heart to pity—
which *did* fill the One great Heart of Infinite
Charity with tenderness and compassion,
although Fluffy knew it not.

Never perhaps before had his mother's
welcome sounded so unwelcome to Charlie
Murphy's ear.

"Well, my lad, did you see anything of
the little boy?" she asked, and Charlie
answered no, so ungraciously, so almost sullenly, that Mrs. Murphy gazed in astonish-
ment at her son.

"You're tired and disappointed, dear,"
she said, pouring him out a smoking cup of
tea. "Don't you be cast down, Charlie.
Why, Our Blessed Lord is just as pleased
you've tried to do something for Him as if
you'd succeeded. You'll light upon the

little chap one of these days no doubt."

There was an awkward silence, in which Charlie was having an uncomfortable tussle with conscience; but he wasn't a mean, deceitful boy, and he could not bear to sit there sipping his hot tea, whilst his mother pitied the fatigue caused by a hunt after Fluffy.

"Mother, I don't know how I could, but I went off with Den Smith," he said, getting it out very fast. "I'll look for the little fellow the first thing to-morrow."

For a moment Mrs. Murphy scarcely seemed to take in his meaning; when she did, an expression came upon her face which Charlie remembered for many and many a day, it was one of such great, bitter disappointment!

"Don't look so, mother; I know you're

angry, and I'm sorry enough now. I've wished Den at Jericho all the afternoon, only ——" and Charlie paused, feeling that no excuse would take that look from his mother's face.

"I'm not angry," she said quietly. "It's only this, Charlie, and I'm right in saying it out if it hurts you ever so. I know you're but young, and one can't expect too much from young folks. All the same I thought that once you knew a thing was right, and something God wanted of you, why you'd do it, let what might be said to hinder you. That's my notion of a good Catholic. Well, it seems to me that you haven't even been hindered or tempted to go against your duty—you just thought of pleasing yourself, and I'm disappointed in you, Charlie."

"Yes, mother, I know, but I'll do it to-morrow."

"I hope you will, but it won't be the same thing. There were no 'to-morrows' with the Lord Jesus Christ when there was some one poor, or sick, or sorrowful, wanting Him. Perhaps I'm hard on you, Charlie, but it's because you've gone right against what you knew God wanted, and it's no wonder I'm disappointed."

*Hard on him!* yes, she was ; so ran Charlie Murphy's thoughts the greater part of the evening, and Fluffy's need was such a sore point that he hurried off to bed before his father returned, lest he, too, might re-open the subject they had talked of at dinner-time.

Charlie's heart was hot and angry then, but after awhile he felt better, when kneeling before his crucifix he had accused himself of all the faults of the day, and asked pardon of God and strength to do better. Next morning he woke up with one strong purpose in his mind, from which, with God's help, nothing should deter him. He would hunt far and near for this poor, friendless, homeless "Fluffy," and do good to him if he could.

# CHAPTER VI.

WE left the young "jail-bird" at a street corner, from whence he listened to Charlie Murphy's quick footsteps, growing more and more indistinct, until at last the trim boyish figure was lost to sight. Fluffy heaved a sigh. It had been pleasant to talk to another lad, even if he was clean and respectable, and different to himself; and the pleasure was over.

What a long day it seemed. It was about nine o'clock when he came out of prison, and now it was barely one; and yet it appeared a whole week at least since those great gates had opened to turn him out

again into the world. What a time it was
too until evening, even though, being winter,
the days closed in early; and then, when
night did come, what should he do and
where should he go?

To sleep on a door-step seemed no great
hardship to Fluffy when the summer sky was
over his head, and the air, if cool, was soft;
now, he shivered in his rags at the thought
of the piercing wind of a frosty January
night, of a policeman turning his bull's-cyc
lantern full upon him and rousing him from
an uneasy sleep to "move on."

For a little while he forgot his riches;
it was such a natural thing to be possessed
of nothing, that Fluffy positively had lost
sight of the fact that he owned the sum of
two shillings and fourpence. The extra
threepence he did not reckon, for he was
going to expend that now at the very next

'shop he came to, for, having digested the sausage-rolls long ago, he was growing hungry.

Door-steps indeed! No need to resort to them while he had money. Not far off there was a slum he knew well, where in a cellar any one who chose might shelter for the payment of twopence. There then he made his way, when the long afternoon and evening had passed, and it was really time to think of sleep. Fluffy had often been kicked and fought with by bigger boys at this and other such places of lodging : but he did not feel afraid, as he used to do. Hadn't he been taken up and committed, and wouldn't the very roughest and worst of them encourage and applaud him if he told that? Ah, and he *would* tell too; he wasn't ashamed of it either, excepting when the chaplain at the prison had told him of

One Who saw him always, or when he was in the company of such as that bright-faced Charlie Murphy, by whose side he had walked that day.

Thus ran Fluffy's thoughts as he trotted along to the lodging he remembered so well, and worse thoughts came afterwards.

Lying on the thin layer of straw which was spread upon the dirty floor, he forgot all about his promise to Mr. Morton, at the prison; forgot the story of Christ, the crucified. He planned all manner of daring robberies which he would effect. In imagination he dived successfully into the pockets of rich gentlemen in the city and elegant ladies in Regent-street, and regaled himself upon unlimited tripe, sausages, baked potatoes, and other articles of diet for which he had a special fancy. Thus thinking, thus planning, Fluffy fell asleep, to dream of jail, chaplain, warder, Joe Rogers, and Charlie Murphy, all mixed up in one great confusion. With the early dawn of morning he went out into the still quiet streets, not having exchanged a word with one of the inmates of the cellar, all of whom were still fast asleep.

Fluffy had a lonely half-scared feeling when he found himself in the silent streets —silent, all but for the footsteps of some man going to his work, or the policeman's heavy tread, or perhaps a milkman beginning his early rounds. To him, the street boy, there was something pleasant and familiar in the noise and confusion which reigns in London during the day and the earlier part of night, and the quiet solitude subdued and almost frightened him. Here and there he lighted upon some wretched woman lying intoxicated on a door-step, unable to reach her home, or some shivering half-starved child; and when he did so it seemed to cheer him, for he did not feel so helplessly alone.

What would Fluffy have felt had he only known that in the early grey light some one was rising quietly but quickly, to go out in search of him—even Charlie Murphy, his acquaintance of the previous day?

In and out of all streets where it was possible he might see Fluffy, round corners, down narrow turnings, back again to the lamp-post at which they parted—yet not a glimpse could Charlie get of the ragged boy he sought. Now and then as his quick eyes caught sight of some forlorn figure with trousers jagged about the ankles, and a rough mop of close-cropped hair, Charlie's heart beat faster with delight, only to be cast down as he discovered his mistake.

He thought that perhaps it was worth while inquiring at some of the smaller shops which now began to open, whether they had seen one such as Fluffy lingering about during the afternoon of the previous day, but on consideration he felt sure that dirty homeless street boys were too common in those parts for anybody to take special heed of one.

He went home at last, weary of his vain search. "Oh, if I had but gone yesterday," he said to himself again and again; but, alas for Charlie Murphy and for us all, no wishes will bring back an opportunity once lost.

God, however, gave him another. It was growing foggy as evening drew on, yet Charlie had gone out again to look for Fluffy. Not with much hope of finding him though—it was more to try and ease his uncomfortable feelings of regret that the boy wandered in and out of his home that day, and could not even be won by Denis Smith to join in any amusement. So it was evening; he had listened to the different churches striking five o'clock, and he had watched the street lamps lighted one by one, and now he stood just where he had parted with Fluffy the day before, only this time he had wandered there almost unconsciously and without any thought of success in his hitherto fruitless search.

Presently he was attracted by the sight of a group of boys, all apparently gathered round two dogs which had been set on to fight.

" At him, good fellow—s-s-s ! Ain't he a plucky un ? Go it, Boxer—at him again !" These were the sounds which reached Charlie's ear and roused his indignation. He was a strong fellow, quite a match for

bigger lads than these cowardly little raga-
muffins. Into the midst of them ran Charlie,
administering sundry cuffs right and left
with hearty good-will.

" You little rascals," he cried, " I'll teach
you better than to set those poor animals on
to fight like that. Be off now every one of
you, or I'll hand you over to the police."

They fell back at this unexpected attack
and disclosed two miserable-looking street
curs, round which they had formed a
ring, as the animals fought, and bit, and
struggled together. One soft hiss of encou-
ragement, one half-muttered "At him !" came
from just one boy, in spite of Charlie's presence and Charlie's threats ; and seizing him
by the collar, preparatory to administering a
good shaking, he found he had secured the
very object of his search—even Fluffy !

" It's you, is it ?" said Charlie, holding the

astonished boy at arm's length, and yet in a tight firm grasp.

" I didn't think you were a coward and a sneak, when I saw you yesterday, and gave you that threepenny bit."

Fluffy remembered him then, and a sense of shame he rarely felt stole over him, as he met the other lad's flashing eyes. The group had dispersed, and Fluffy was left alone with Charlie, for his new-made acquaintances preferred getting out of the reach of such very vigorous interference with their amusements.

"Who do those dogs belong to?" demanded Charlie, giving Fluffy a slight shake.

"I dunno," was the reply. " The other chaps was round 'em when I came up. I was only a-lookin' on at the fun."

"*Fun!*" exclaimed Charlie, giving his prisoner another shake. "Let me catch you or any one else at such 'fun' again, and I'll make you remember it. I'll give you such a thrashing that——"

"You're nothin' better nor a bully, a great big bully," interrupted Fluffy. "Can't a feller have a bit of fun without *you* a-interferin' with what ain't your bisness?"

"It *is* my business," said Charlie angrily. "It's everybody's business to stop such cowardly, hateful games as dog-fighting. And I'm not a bully either—you might hit me and I'd not take the trouble to give it back to a little chap less than my own size, and *that's* what a bully 'd do. But I'll thrash you if I catch you at this sort of work again, I warn you," and with another shake he released his victim.

For a moment the two boys looked at each other, then Charlie spoke: "I'm sorry if I've hurt you, Fluffy. I'm apt not to be over-gentle when my blood's up, and that's the sort of thing that rouses me."

"Oh, I ain't so easy hurt," replied the other scornfully. "You thinks a mighty deal of yourself, but you're not so very much bigger than me, as you calls a little chap. I knows a cove what 'd make nothin' of knockin' you down, big swell as you are."

"I'm not a big swell," said Charlie, trying to keep down his wrath; "I told you yesterday what I was. I'm not so very different to you, except that I've had a good home and good parents, and have been better brought up."

"What do you know of my bringin's up?" retorted Fluffy, still inclined to be quarrelsome.

"Well, not much," said Charlie goodhumouredly. "I'd like to know all about you, Fluffy; I'd like us to be friends too."

"Friends!" muttered the other boy. "*Friends!*" and you a-grippin' of me by the collar, and a-shakin' of me like that! You've tore my jacket worse'nt was before, I b'lieve;" and Fluffy took a side-glance over his shoulder to see if he could detect an additional rent to the many which already adorned his garments.

"No, I don't think *I've* torn it," said Charlie. "But look here, Fluffy, I'll give you another that hasn't got so much as a slit, though it is a bit worn. You come along as far as where I live, and I'll give you that."

"Shan't!" said the boy, setting his back firmly against the wall by which they were now standing; nevertheless, there was a look in his eyes which told that he would have been well pleased to accept Charlie's offer had not some feeling of mistrust possessed

him ; and, in spite of all the other lad could
do or say, he persisted in this refusal.

" Why won't you come, Fluffy? it isn't
far," said Charlie as persuasively as he
could.

" 'Cause I won't," said Fluffy ; " I'd have
come yesterday, when you spoke to me
civil.  I won't come now, and you may keep
your   old   jacket   yourself   for   all   I
cares."

" No, I won't keep it ; I'll bring it to
you, Fluffy, if you can tell me where to find
you—say at eight to-morrow morning."

" I might be somewhere about here, I
can't exactly say," replied the other, who
was delighted at the idea, though he managed
to keep up an indifferent manner still.

" Well, good-night," said Charlie, at last,
feeling somewhat discouraged by this, his
first attempt to do a kind and good action ;

7

" I'll come and look if you are anywhere in this part to-morrow morning."

Thus they parted : Fluffy to regale himself with some baked potatoes before seeking his night's lodging ; Charlie to think more and more regretfully of his failure.

" He said he'd have come yesterday, and perhaps he would," so ran his thoughts. "I wish I'd gone after him then ; but there, wishing is no use. I wonder if I was rough with him just now. I didn't mean it ; but I can't endure such sports with those wretched brutes of street dogs. Well, I must try and get round the little chap yet !" and when Charlie told his adventures to his mother, she kept him up to this resolution.

" Never mind if it's hard, Charlie," she said. " 'Tis worth a bit of difficulty if you can do him some good in the end. I'd say a Hail Mary for the boy to-night if I were you; it's sure to do him good, and it'll keep your own spirits up to try again after him to-morrow,"

# CHAPTER VII.

THE fog of the previous night had all cleared off; already there were signs betokening a fine day, early though it was—one of those bright sunny days which almost make us forget that many keen winds and drifting snow storms lie between us and the sweet spring time.

Early as Fluffy had been stirring the day before, he was still earlier now, for his head was full of Charlie Murphy and the promised jacket.

Eight o'clock had been the hour appointed; but as the clocks struck seven any one who had passed the corner of a certain

back street in Westminster might have seen
a ragged pale-faced boy peering anxiously
into the dusky light, as if trying to catch
the first glimpse of something he waited
for.

"I don't s'pose he'll bring along that
there jacket," said Fluffy in an undertone
every now and then—perhaps he was trying
to prepare himself for disappointment, if
disappointment came, for certainly he was
both watching and hoping for Charlie Murphy's arrival, and something seemed to as-
sure him that Charlie was a boy who would
keep his promise.

It was just five minutes after eight when
he came in sight, breathless and running.

"Here you are then, Fluffy" he said,
panting very much from the haste he had
been making. "Here you are, and here's
your jacket."

Fluffy reached out both hands for the garment, and held it up admiringly.

"My! ain't it a reg'lar stunner," he exclaimed; and then, divesting himself of his rags, he had it on in a twinkling, to his own and Charlie's satisfaction.

"Why, I'll turn out a reg'lar swell myself, and no mistake," he said, turning round and taking a survey of himself as best he could in the nearest shop window. "I must give myself a bit of a rinse though, now I've got this 'ere stunnin' jacket."

"Well, I think it *would* be an improvement," said Charlie; "you've not caught sight of any soap and water lately, I'm thinking."

"Well, no; not for a day or so," said Fluffy candidly. "You wait till to-morrow; I'll be off to them fountains afore the p'lice is about, and get a bit of this grime off."

Charlie looked somewhat astonished, but said nothing.

"I thought you wasn't a-coming," proceeded Fluffy, who seemed to have forgotten his resentment of the previous night; "you was after eight."

"Only a minute or two," replied Charlie; "I couldn't help it. It's my week to serve Mass at seven o'clock, and then I had to cut round home to fetch the jacket."

"Serve what?" questioned Fluffy.

"Mass. I dare say you don't know what that is. It's a service at our church in the mornings."

"What's your church?" said Fluffy looking hard at the elder boy.

"My church! Why, the Catholic one, over there," and he indicated some place towards the right.

"Oh, I knows," responded Fluffy with an

experienced air. "I knows Irishers are mostly Catholics. I knows the church too, and I've seen the folks a-goin in Sundays. I've taken a look in myself too, and seen 'eaps and 'eaps of candles, and flowers, and pictures, and all the rest of it. So you goes there ?"

"Yes," said Charlie, "I go there Sundays, and week days too, very often."

But Fluffy had returned to the admiration of his jacket as a more interesting matter.

"I'm much obliged to you, I am," he said. "This'll keep the cold out fine when I goes to work."

"What work do you try?" said Murphy, hoping to get a little information as to Fluffy's way of life.

"Well, I'm not pertikler; anything as comes 'andy. I s'pose you don't know of any shop where they wants a boy ?"

The other lad considered a moment.

" I don't know," he said at length ; " perhaps mother does. If you'll come as far as our place, you might ask her."

Fluffy whistled. Evidently there was some attraction in the idea, and yet he was not altogether willing. But Charlie took advantage of his hesitation, and pressed him so hard that presently they were walking along together towards the street where the Murphys lived.

" I'd been looking for you all yesterday, Fluffy," said Charlie ; " I'd almost given you up when I came upon you with those boys."

" Ah, they're a bad lot ; awful bad," said Fluffy, as calmly as if he had had no dealings with them. " What was you a-looking after me for ?"

" Well, I wanted you to come along and

have something to eat at our place, for one thing," said Charlie. " And then I thought that jacket would come in handy, and besides I wanted to know how you were getting on without any parents to help you."

" Bless your heart ! they wasn't no help to me," said Fluffy earnestly. " That's to say father wasn't. He were allers given to drink and bad ways afore he took hisself off, which were a blessin', as mother used to say."

" And did your mother drink too ?" asked Charlie.

" No," said Fluffy. " She weren't give to drinkin'. She were a poor creatur—thin and weak like, and at last she couldn't go to the laundry-work no more, and next thing she died." He spoke in an unconcerned way, as if it was some matter in which he had no personal feeling, yet deep down in his heart was a tender spot which Charlie Murphy could not see, and that was a sort of love and longing for his dead mother.

"Had she got any religion?" asked Charlie, pondering over this description of the poor woman's death; then seeing that Fluffy did not understand him, he added, "Did ever any priest, any clergyman, come to see her?"

"Bless you no!" ejaculated Fluffy, in great surprise. "Whatever 'd be the use of it? She didn't want no one a comin' to see her. She wanted good vittles, so the doctor said, and as she couldn't have 'em she died. But she were a rare long time afore she went off."

Charlie was silent—this was a state of things he hardly knew how to deal with.

"Where did your mother live?" he asked, after a pause.

"Dockett's-buildings, as I told you afore," said Fluffy, "T'aint a very nice sort of place, but there's worser. I don't live there now, though."

"You've never told me yet where you do live," said Charlie.

"When my visitin' cards is printed I'll give you one," said Fluffy, who occasionally tried to say something he thought witty, after the pattern of Joe Rogers and other lads he had come across. But hardly had he spoken the words than he added, "I don't live nowheres just now. I stops in the streets best part of the day, and at night I gets a lodging where I can.".

"Well, I hope you'll soon get to work," said Charlie. "Here we are at home, and here's mother."

Yes; there was the cheerful face in the doorway, for Mrs. Murphy had seen the two boys coming, and now she held out her hand to the dirty little stray who stood by Charlie's side.

He did not take it though ; perhaps such civilities had never come under his notice in Dockett's-buildings. He stood downcast before the kind face and searching eyes, his one sole comfort that he had arrayed himself in Charlie's tidy jacket.

"So this is Fluffy," said Mrs. Murphy pleasantly. "I'm very glad to see you, my lad. Step in."

Fluffy hesitated ; in spite of the jacket he was conscious of other deficiencies in his appearance which those bright keen eyes must discern.

"I'm not so clean as might be," he said, glancing at his dirty hands, and remembering what his face had looked like as he saw it reflected in the shop windows.

"Never mind that just now," said Mrs. Murphy. "You must come and have a bit of breakfast along with my Charlie. He wouldn't sit down to anything, but was off after you the minute he came from church."

Fluffy said nothing, but he thought a great deal of those words—to put off breakfast until the promised jacket had been bestowed was a piece of self-denial and good-will which he was quite able to comprehend. He sat down awkwardly on the edge of the chair which Mrs. Murphy pushed towards the bright fire.

His wonder and admiration at the pretty, tidy room, were such that he felt himself like a blot or stain upon it all, and the strangeness of his situation almost frightened him.

Oh, why had he ever let this Charlie "come over" him and bring him in his dirt and misery to this clean bright home where he was so out of place? Yet in spite of this feeling there was some pleasure to Fluffy in being there; it would be a fine thing to think of at night when he was wet and cold and hungry.

Meanwhile Mrs. Murphy had pushed up the table to the fire and put upon it two plates, two knives and forks, cups, saucers, and all things necessary for a comfortable breakfast. There were herrings, too, toasting—the very smell of which raised Fluffy's spirits. If only he had got his "bit of a rinse" that morning how he would have enjoyed it all.

"Perhaps you'd take your breakfast more comfortable if you was to go into our back-kitchen and have a wash," said Mrs. Murphy, as if she read his thoughts. "Go with him, Charlie, and I'll be ready for you by the time you're ready for me."

Fluffy did not hesitate over this invitation, and when he returned, his hands and face were very clean, and he looked altogether improved by his ablutions.

Now and then Fluffy had indulged in a breakfast at one of the coffee-stalls, but even that was surpassed by the plentiful meal Mrs. Murphy put before him, for in her kind heart she had determined he should satisfy his hunger now, if need be, for the rest of the day.

After a few minutes the boy's first shyness wore off, but he still remained very quiet and was in great difficulty about conveying the herring to his mouth with a knife and fork, after the example of Charlie—in Dockett's-buildings people were more primitive in habits and made use of their fingers upon such occasions.

However, he got on fairly well considering

it was a first attempt, and although he dropped some of the most tempting morsels on the floor which he had intended putting elsewhere, he managed to make a very excellent breakfast.

" Don't go yet," said Charlie, as Fluffy made signs of shuffling towards the door. " It's holidays, so I've nothing particular to do. Wouldn't you like to see how nice that book-shelf looks that you carried home for me ? Here it is, behind the door, and those are all my books."

Fluffy gazed at the wall and the books, but said nothing.

" Can you read ?" asked Mrs. Murphy, as she began clearing the table.

" Well, I'm not to say a scholard," said Fluffy, modestly. " I can make out a word here and there if the print's a fair size; I've never had no schoolin' you see, mum; it was mother as learned me all I knows."

"And she is dead, is she?" said Mrs. Murphy. "Poor boy, it's very lonesome for you."

It was not the words, but the tone of her voice which made Fluffy turn and look at her—then brush his hand across his eyes. Pity was so new to him that it touched that one soft corner in his heart, and in Mrs. Murphy's voice there was pity so deep and so real that even Fluffy felt its influence.

"Yes, it's lonesome," he said, in a choked, husky voice, which sounded strangely unlike his own; but the emotion passed, and with a jerk of his thumb towards one of the pictures on the wall, he enquired what it was.

"That is Our Lord, crowned with thorns," said Charlie; "and this is Our Lady and the

Holy Child, and that one over the fire-place is St. Joseph, and——" but Mrs. Murphy stopped any further description.

"He can't remember if you tell him so many names at once, Charlie. You like that one, don't you, Fluffy?"

"Yes, I likes it 'cause I can make it out a bit. I've heard of him a-wearin' them thorns, the chaplain—he told me." And there a terrible confusion seized Fluffy. Had he betrayed himself? Would that kind-faced woman with the pleasant voice guess he was a jail-bird and never let him come inside her bright parlour any more?

For an instant the boy looked at Charlie and at his mother; but neither of them appeared to have understood what he said or to notice his alarm.

"I'm glad you have heard of it," said.

Mrs. Murphy, quietly; "it's a beautiful picture."

"Yes, m'm. I'll be going now, if you please," said Fluffy, fearing another slip of the tongue. "Good-bye, mum, and thank you."

"Well, good-bye, Fluffy, for to-day, but mind you come again. Come round this way to-morrow, if you can," she answered; and Charlie held out his hand and said he should look out for him, so that Fluffy took his leave in a great state of delight. He had more than half made up his mind to visit Dockett's-buildings and give a description of that breakfast to an admiring and envious audience, but on second thoughts he decided to keep away from "that low part," for a new desire had sprung up from that first visit to Mrs. Murphy's neat home, and that desire was to be respectable and tidy too.

# CHAPTER VIII.

IT was not a very easy matter for Fluffy to decide how that wish of his could possibly be realised. He knew full well that "respectable" people never went about dirty or tattered, neither did they sleep in cellars away in the slums and alleys of London, nor did they loiter about the streets unemployed. All these habits and customs were his, and he had never thought of changing them until that one visit to the Murphys' dwelling.

The bright chintz curtains at the window, the neatly papered walls, covered as they were almost with pictures, the fresh cleanli-

ness of everything had done its work, and
even the hyacinth which stood on a little
table seemed to tell Fluffy that there was a
higher, better way of life than any he had as
yet known, and that dirt, misery, and sin,
were out of keeping with such surroundings.

He could not very well have put his
feelings into words, but a longing had come
up in his heart to be such an one as Charlie
Murphy; to have a pleasant home, and keep
clear of pocket-picking, policemen, and
prisons.   In the filthy cellar, his one ambition had seemed to be that of becoming
a successful and clever thief—in the tidy
working-man's home he felt the shame of
such a career, and bad, hardening thoughts
left him, and he longed to get out of the
uncertain dangerous way in which his feet
were walking.

"I may wish, and wish, but 'taint no

use," he muttered, as he went his way in and out of one street after another, just to pass the time.

"What is no use?" said a pleasant voice close by his side, for Fluffy had spoken louder than he intended and had been overheard. Somewhat startled, he would have given a saucy reply, only something in the face of the gentleman who spoke hindered him. "What is no use?—make haste and tell me," he said again quickly, yet kindly.

"Nothing's no use," said Fluffy, looking very foolish.

"Now that is a stupid answer, and I don't think you are a stupid boy," was the reply. "What were you talking about to yourself? I don't like to see a little fellow like you giving up things that way."

"It's fine talking," said Fluffy, no longer

afraid. " If *you* was me I'd lay anything *you'd* say just what I says."

" Perhaps I should, so tell me all about it, my boy."

" It's only as I'd like to be decent and respectable, same as Charlie Murphy, and I don't see my way to it. That's not much to tell."

"Oh, do you know Charley Murphy? I know him too—you mean a bright lad that lives in yonder street with his father and mother, do you?"

" Yes, that's him," said Fluffy gazing in the direction to which the stranger pointed. " Number 'leven, I b'lieves it is. Yes, I know him."

" Well, why shouldn't you be respectable? Have you got good parents?'

" Haven't got none," said the boy.

" A good aunt, or sister, or some one to look after you then?"

"Haven't got none of 'em," said Fluffy again; "I takes care of myself best way I can."

"Ah, that is a hard matter," said the stranger, seriously. "A very hard matter for a boy like you. But even then, don't say it is no use wishing to be good and respectable."

"I didn't say nothin' about *good*," explained Fluffy. "I'd like a clean place to live in and plenty to eat; but *good* means church goin' and that sort of thing, as I don't care for, nor never shall."

"Then you can't be like Charlie Murphy," said the gentleman, decidedly. "I'll tell you why he and his parents are so comfortable and happy. It is because they try to please and serve God, and so God blesses them and their work and prospers them." There was silence for a minute, and then looking into the boy's face, the stranger said, " Do you know what I mean ? Do you know anything about God ?"

"Oh yes, I've heerd tell of *Him*," answered Fluffy, promptly ; " lives up there," and he jerked his thumb in the direction of the chimney-pots and roofs of houses.

" Come, that is something to know. Did you ever hear that He sees all you do ?"

" Yes, I've heerd that too," replied Fluffy.

" And do you ever think of it when you are out about in the streets ? Does it make you afraid to do wrong ?"

" Well no, I can't rightly say it do," said Fluffy. " 'Taint altogether pleasant to think on, so I mostly forgets it."

There was a smile upon the kind face, though a smile which had no merriment in it, and Fluffy observing it, felt more inclined to cry than to laugh, though he did not know why.

"Poor boy!" said the stranger. "I should like to help you to feel differently towards God; I should like to help you to understand what a good friend He wants to be to you, if you would only let Him."

"Oh, I'll let Him," said Fluffy; "I wants friends bad enough, for since I've broke with Joe Rogers I don't know no one to speak to—except Murphy, and I only see him yesterday."

"But listen to this, my boy. God can't be a friend to you if you don't think of Him and try to do what would please Him."

"I don't know nothin' about pleasin' Him," said Fluffy, sullenly.

"Is that true?" and the pleasant kindly face was turned towards him, to Fluffy's great confusion.

"Well, I only know what Mr. Morton told me. He's a — a parson," said the boy, hesitating very much.

"And what did he tell you?"

"He told me as God lived up in heaven, and people was so desperate wicked He didn't know how to put up with it as I may say. And then, He made Hisself like a man, and called Hisself Christ Jesus and come down and lived here—lived hard like the poor, though I don't think I heard nothin' of His bein' dirty and ragged, like some of 'em."

"Well, what more have you heard?"

"I heard as how at last they made a end of Him. Nailed him on a wooden cross and let Him die, and that's all."

"And all that is true; you believe it, don't you?"

"Yes, I b'lieves it. In course I couldn't

go for to think Mr. Morton 'd make it up
out of his head."

"Doesn't it make you want to be a good
boy when you know all that?"

"Sometimes it do, and sometimes it
don't," said Fluffy. "Mr. Morton, he told
me as if I b'lieved it all, and b'lieved that
my sins was forgive me because of Him
dyin' so, I'd be saved and go to heaven, but
I can't feel as *that's* true."

"Why not?" said the gentleman.

"'Cause it don't seem like it," said Fluffy.
"If I were a-goin so sure to heaven I'd feel
a bit different to what I do. I knows as
it's the good sort of folks what go to heaven
—not anyone like me."

"And what makes people good?"

"Mr. Morton said as believin' all that
made 'em good; but it hasn't made no sort
of difference in me."

"I'll tell you why," said Fluffy's new friend. "All that you have been told is true, but it is not the *whole* truth. There is more for you to learn than that. You must believe Christ died to save you, but, besides that, there is something for you to *do*. You must get your sins washed clean away, and then begin a new life, with God to help you."

Fluffy's face brightened. "Ah, that would be somethin' like," he said. "If I could get rid of all I've done, and begin clean, and fresh, and respectable, it would be fine. But that's not to be done, and the b'lieving don't seem no good to such as me."

"If I tell you it *is* to be done, and that you can get free of all the sin you ever did— just as free as a little child who has not done anything wrong—should you think it was true?"

Fluffy hesitated, and took a glance at his companion. "I most thinks you're a parson, ain't you?" he said.

"Well, not exactly. I am a priest, if you know what that is."

"Oh, yes, I knows. It's the same sort of thing. You preaches in church, and gives out hymns, and all the rest of it. I knows."

"Well, I want to hear if you think what I tell you now is true."

Fluffy hesitated. "Supposin' you was to tell me how it's done p'r'aps it'd seem more likely then."

"That I will; and I can tell you besides that all through these hundreds and hundreds of years since Christ died on the Cross, there have been men, women, and little children getting their sins cleansed away, all over the world, and every day and week, and month."

"My goodness!" ejaculated Fluffy. "It's a pity some of them folks in Dockett's-buildins' didn't never get it done. P'r'aps you don't know that part, Mister? It's orful low, it is. That's where I used to live, along of mother."

"No, I don't think I ever was in a place of that name. Where have you been living since?"

"Oh, here, and there, and everywhere!" said Fluffy, fencing the question.

"I think I can guess something about you. There is a Mr. Morton I used to know years ago, who is a chaplain at a prison. Isn't that one of the places you have been in?"

A red glow suffused Fluffy's face, but he did not deny it.

"What if I have? There's lots more as have been there too besides me."

" Yes, that is very true ; and I am sure you will try not to go there again, will you not ?"

" If I can get any work," said the boy. " I must live somehow."

" Suppose you let me help you a bit. You say you have not got any friends, so you must take me for one. Is it a bargain ?"

Fluffy nodded his head, and looked delighted.

" Very well; then you had better come in with me now, and let us think what is to be done for you. I live here," and Fluffy's new-made friend stopped at the door of a house they had just reached.

But the boy hesitated, and coloured, and at last said, " I'd like you to know just what sort I am, afore you does anything to help me. I've lived very low, and I've thieved and swore, and done all manner of things as decent folks don't do. Then I took to picking the gentlemen's pockets till a p'liceman nabbed me, and I got three months for it. I've only just come out of jail, and I've lived in the streets these two days."

He brought it all out very rapidly and with downcast eyes, as if he did not want to see that kind face grow shocked and stern. Oh, what a surprise to Fluffy when he felt a hand laid gently on his shoulder, drawing him in at the already opened door.

"I have heard many such tales, and even worse ones," said the priest. "It is just such boys as you I want to find and to help. Come in here; you know I am to be your friend now, and I have promised to tell you how you are to get rid of all the past, and begin a good and honest life."

## CHAPTER IX.

THERE was service at the church that evening, and as Charlie Murphy donned his cassock and prepared to go upon the altar, he thought he heard some peculiar noise coming from a distant corner of the sacristy —*so* peculiar that he and the other boys who were there stared at each other in round-eyed amazement.

" It's nothing," said little Riley, and they resumed their whispered conversation— *whispered*, because there was a great "Silence" framed upon the sacristy wall, which they seldom regarded in any other way than by lowering their voices.

But surely such a decided "his-sis-is"
could not come from "nothing," and proceeding to search that corner of the sacristy,
a boy was found with bright eyes and short-
cropped hair, clean face and hands, and
tidy, if worn clothing, who yet bore a
wonderful likeness to our friend Fluffy.

"Now you just let a feller alone, can't
you?" he said, struggling in the midst of the
boys, who had gathered round him, demand-
ing what he was doing there. "I don't
want nothin' of any of you 'cept Charlie
Murphy there. He's a friend of mine!"

"Charlie, here's a young gentleman of
your acquaintance," said Riley—for Charlie
was a little apart from the group.

"A friend of mine! I don't know him
then," said the lad carelessly. "Are you
waiting here for one of the priests?"

"No, I ain't," said Fluffy promptly;

"I'm a-waitin' here for you, to tell you of my good luck."

"Me! Why I never set eyes on you before," exclaimed Charlie, in evident surprise.

"Well, if that ain't cuttin' a feller dead!" ejaculated Fluffy, turning to the rest. "You'd never b'lieve as his mother asked me to breakfast no longer ago than this blessed mornin'."

"My mother—asked you?" and Charlie gazed in a bewildered way at the boy, whom he could only see indistinctly in the dim light of that corner of the sacristy. "Come out and let's have a look at you! Why, if it isn't Fluffy!"

"Yes, it's me," said the other, chuckling with delight, and then, suddenly recollecting where he was, assuming an air of great seriousness. "What a noise you chaps are a-makin'," he said reprovingly; "you'll have one of them parsons after you if you don't shut up."

There was a subdued titter, but as a step approached the door leading into the presbytery which was well-known to be that of one of the "parsons" the dialogue ended abruptly, and Fluffy disappeared in the shade from which he had been drawn, while the others put on their cottas and . composed their faces to a proper gravity as Father Dunstan appeared to take his part in the service.

I dare say all the boys had some few distractions that evening in remembering the appearance of Fluffy, but no one was so puzzled as Charlie Murphy. How had the street-boy found his way there, and how and by whom had he been transformed into almost a respectable being ?

All these difficulties were solved after the

Benediction service, when Father Dunstan called Murphy aside.

" You know something of a lad who calls himself Fluffy, I think ?"

" Yes, Father."

" Well, tell me all you can about him."

So Charlie told the history of their first meeting and the search he had neglected and afterwards made ; of Fluffy's refusal to go to his home, and later, of his visit there only that morning.

" Well, I am glad to see he is truthful thus far," said Father Dunstan. " His story is much the same as yours. I want you now to go on with the good work you have begun, Charlie ; you must help Fluffy to be a Christian boy."

" Oh, I haven't begun any good work, Father," said Charlie shyly. " Mother put me up to looking for him and saying a kind word to him, poor little chap. I *was* astonished to see him in here, Father."

"In here?" repeated Father Dunstan, upon which Charlie related what had happened.

The priest laughed. " I thought I had got him safely in my kitchen, filling scuttles and doing odds and ends for the housekeeper, until we can put him to work. I suppose he was looking for you. Did you tell him you were a Catholic ?"

" Oh yes, Father, and he seemed to understand."

" I am coming round to your house now to see if your mother can take him in tonight," said Father Dunstan ; " you may as well walk with me."

Charlie obeyed, but as he stepped out by the priest's side a vexed feeling was in his heart. Was not Father Dunstan expecting too much if he thought mother ought to take in a little scamp out of the street? It was all very well to find him an old jacket or so, and even to give him a breakfast—Charlie could get over *that;* but to have him an inmate of their nice clean home —well, he didn't like it a bit, and he hoped mother would get out of it. That was how Charlie Murphy felt, and Father Dunstan seemed to guess partly what was in his mind, for there was a gleam of amusement in his eye as he looked at the boy beside him.

" You know your Catechism, do you not, Charlie ?"

" Yes, Father."

" Then you can easily tell me the corporal works of Mercy."

In a somewhat unwilling voice, and as fast as he could, Charlie repeated them.

" It *is* sometimes a hard thing to put what we have learnt into practice, is it not?"

said the priest, now quite serious. "And
yet if we belong to our Lord, and do not
wish Him to be ashamed of us in the last
great day, we must do it. *He* was not
above being in the company of the poorest
and lowest—even the most sinful, Charlie;
and I am quite sure that if He dwelt upon
the earth now He would take such a poor,
friendless lad as Fluffy to His own home and
bid him welcome."

Charlie said nothing. It was all true, he
knew it as well as the priest himself, and believed it equally, and yet—well, I suppose he
was considering what "all the fellows" of
his acquaintance would say if there was such
a young scapegrace as Fluffy quartered in
their house; one of the best homes of any
of the working-class of that neighbourhood.

Mrs. Murphy was too kindly disposed to
refuse to do what the priest asked her,

though for a moment it cost her a struggle. "I'll make him up a bed in the kitchen, Father, if that will do," she said. "I couldn't put him with Charlie—one never knows what these street-boys are, and I've always kept my lad respectable."

"Quite right," replied the priest. "I shall be well satisfied and very glad if you can put Fluffy in the back-kitchen, and I am sure he has never yet been so comfortably lodged. I hope to see more clearly what to do with him in the course of another day."

"Go with his reverence, Charlie, and bring the boy," said Mrs. Murphy, and Charlie went—still slightly unwilling; nevertheless, as he returned through the streets with Fluffy by his side, he could not help taking an interest in his ungenteel companion, which soon dispelled the annoyance he had felt.

"I think I must 'ave been born with a silver spoon in *my* mouth, as the sayin' is," said Fluffy, as the two boys left the priest's house. "Only to think of my fallin' in with your parson, and him a-takin' such a fancy to me."

Charlie could not help laughing. "You shouldn't call him a parson; he's a priest, and you'd best remember it."

"Don't be waxy about such a trifle," said Fluffy coolly. "I can't see as one word's better than another, but I'll call him a priest if you're pertic'ler about it. And then he proceeded to give the details of his meeting with Father Dunstan in the morning of that day, which lasted until they reached the Murphys' door.

"Good-evening," said Mrs. Murphy, meeting them, and smiling kindly at Fluffy.

"Good-evenin' to you, mum, and glad to

see you," said Fluffy, who, being now
unwontedly clean and tidy, felt more at
ease than he had done upon the occasion
of his first visit.

But catching sight of Charlie's father,
whom he had not met before, he became
suddenly shy and silent, nor could a word
be got from him while he eat his supper,
although he gazed at them all in turn, and
looked well at everything which the room
contained.

"You're tired, and will be glad to get to
bed, I'm sure," said Mrs. Murphy at last.
"Show him where he's going to sleep,
Charlie."

Never before had Fluffy's eyes beheld
such comfortable arrangements for a night's
rest, and as he stretched out his weary
limbs, and felt the warm coverings which
were laid over him, had any one listened

they would have heard a low sob break
from his lips.  Was he not then happy and
content?  Did the old, rough life possess
some charm which he regretted at this
moment when new ways seemed opening
before his feet?  Oh no! it was not that
which brought the tears to his eyes.  It
was the sense of comfort and the kind-
nees of those who had taken pity on him
which touched and melted Fluffy's heart.
He felt so unworthy of it all, so grateful,
that he determined never to do anything
which such good friends could disapprove.
"It's them better times that's come," this
was his last waking thought.  "They've
come for me, though they didn't come for
mother.  Poor mother! I'd like to think she
knew how comfortable I'm lodged to-night."

## CHAPTER X.

FOR some days Fluffy's time was spent in doing any work which could be found for him at the priest's house, while each evening saw him on his way to the Murphys' house, where he met with a warm welcome from Charlie's mother, even if Charlie himself did not take kindly to the new order of things.

The fact was that it was a little hard for the boy just then to bear with all the remarks his companions had to make on the subject of Fluffy.

"I say, Murphy, how do you get on with young Rags?" one would say; or, "Charlie, have your folks taken in that little beggar for good and all?" "Mother says she wonders how *your* mother can be so easy got over by a low little chap like that." "My father says you'll all be precious sorry you had anything to do with him; you'll find your mistake one of these days."

Such and many more were the opinions showered upon Charlie Murphy, and as he was *only* a boy, with a boy's weaknesses and a boy's sensitiveness to ridicule, we must not judge him hardly if it must be told that he was apt to give Fluffy a wide berth when they came in contact anywhere but in the privacy of the Murphys' house, where there was no one to laugh and no one to condemn.

There, at night—when Mrs. Murphy sat sewing, while she listened for her husband's step coming home from his work—Charlie would read aloud some of his own cherished books for tho amusement of Fluffy, who listened with almost breathless interest and delight.

Sometimes they would get talking about their church and its services, and then Fluffy's ears were widely opened, for he seemed to take a special interest in all that was Catholic, although as yet he was not very well disposed to become a Catholic himself.

"The priest's a-learnin' of me 'most every day," he said to Mrs. Murphy, when the first week of his new life had come to an end. "Bless yer, mum, he's took a rare deal of trouble already, a-makin' of it plain to me that I can get rid of all my bad life, and do better—but I don't know. Sometimes I think it's no good for such as me ; folks that's never been as low as I've lived wouldn't believe as I wanted to keep right.

10

They'd be always a-lookin' at me as if they was suspectin' of me, and none of the boys. here would ever have anything to say to me, 'cause they knows I've not been brought up same as them."

He did not even so much as glance at Charlie; yet Charlie felt that his secret was known—that Fluffy quite understood that he was ashamed of him.

A flush mounted to the boy's forehead, and he bent over his book, as if he was not heeding the conversation, but he caught every word which fell from his mother or from Fluffy.

"No, they wouldn't—not if they were good Catholics," said Mrs. Murphy. "They couldn't go against our Lord like that, my lad. Why if *He* loves the poorest and the lowest, and if *He* likes to have them turn from what's wrong, and never casts it up

against them, you don't suppose that any
one who loves and fears God would dare to
do it either, do you?"

"I'm not a-sayin' it in blame to 'em," said
the boy simply. "I don't see how them
that's respectable could well like to have me
along with 'em. It seems as if I'd do best
with my own sort, only then they're so
desp'rate bad. I don't want to get back
into them bad ways of mine if I can help it."

"You can help it, but not unless you've
God's grace to stand by you. Surely,
Fluffy, you're not going to turn away from
that, when Jesus, Who wore the crown of
thorns for you, is asking you to come
to Him?"

The boy glanced at the picture. "Them
are the sort of things that come over me,"
he said, and his voice faltered. "When
the priest tells me all that Christ Jesus did,

and says it was for me as much as for a
king or a queen, I feels that sorry I'd do
anything; but then when I meets them who
look as if they'd not have any dealings with
me, why then I feel as if it was all no good."

"I'll tell you what to do," said Mrs.
Murphy, leaning on the table, and looking
straight at Fluffy. "Don't you think of
any one but our Lord and His dear Mother.
They are not ashamed of you, nor ever will
be. They *love* you, my boy, and it's that
love which has brought you out of all the
evil which was round you, on purpose that
you might get fit to serve them in this
world and live with them in the next. Just
you say over and over to yourself, ' Jesus
and Mary love me; Jesus and Mary are
waiting for me to begin a new life;' and
then you'll take no heed of what other folks
may feel about you. All the same, Fluffy,

I think it's your fancy that the boys about the church look down on you."

" No, I don't think it's fancy," said Fluffy quietly. " Nor I don't wonder at 'em. I dare say I'd feel much the same myself. But I'll think them words you've said, mum ; p'r'aps they'll do me some good."

Charlie, in his corner by the fire, heard no more after that; his thoughts were turned upon himself.

In that moment, light seemed given him to see into his own heart, and to find there such feelings as he had never imagined he possessed. It dawned upon Charlie then, that he had given way to pride—pride in his good character, in his regular attendance at church, his standing as one of the best boys at school, in fact, pride seemed lurking in all the good actions of his life. And then he remembered the parable of the Pharisee and the publican. Surely, in his own way he had been glorying that he was not such an one as poor Fluffy; he—of whom all thought so well—had been acting the Pharisee!

It was not a pleasant truth which had come home to Charlie's heart, yet it did him good, though it cost him something to keep down that satisfaction with self which the Holy Spirit had enlightened him to see within his heart. Ah! how it cropped up when he thought it conquered; how it twisted and twined itself in and about even his best purposes, and betrayed itself at times and in places where he was least prepared to meet it. That fight lasted Charlie Murphy his lifetime, which he began first in his boyhood, as he listened in the fireside corner to his mother talking with poor Fluffy.

That very evening Charlie struck a blow at the new-found fault. There was Benediction at the church, and he was going upon the altar as usual. When he had put on overcoat and cap, he turned to Fluffy, who was eying him rather wistfully.

" I thought you said you liked the church at nights, Fluffy," he remarked.

" So I does," responded the other. " I likes to see you chaps come in before the priest, and I likes the singing. I watched you all the time that first night I hid up in the corner."

" Why don't you come on now, and stop in the church and hear it all then ?"

" Come along of you !" said Fluffy, scarcely believing his own cars.

" Yes, if you like. You can't come on the altar because you're not a Catholic, but I'll look for you in the church after service."

The two boys went off together, at first in silence; then with an effort, Charlie spoke.

" Fluffy, I'm afraid I've been like that—like you were saying to mother—and I wanted to tell you I'm sorry. You're not going to let me keep you from being a Catholic, are you ? it would make me miserable all my days if I thought that."

" I didn't mean that," said Fluffy ; " that is, not exactly. I meant as I wouldn't like to be a Catholic if folks 'd be ashamed of me."

" I'm afraid you thought I was ashamed of you," said Charlie.

" Well, you was, wasn't you ?" said Fluffy.

" No—yes—that is," and Charlie stammered very much ; " if I have been, Fluffy, I'm not now, and I'm sorry—more sorry than I could ever tell you. You'll not think of it any more, will you ?"

" No, I've promised your mother I'd give up them kind of thoughts, and I mean to try. *She's* never felt anything but kind to me."

"No, mother's too good for that," said Charlie warmly. "You can't think how good she is, Fluffy."

"Ain't all you Catholics good?" asked Fluffy.

"No, indeed. They are, some of them, dreadfully bad, Fluffy."

"Then where's the use of being one?"

"Because it's the only way of pleasing God," said Charlie. "Don't you see, Fluffy, that it isn't *because* they're Catholics that people are bad, it's because they don't do what their religion teaches them. Let them be as bad as they may, that don't alter the Catholic Church."

"Then, them bad ones isn't no better off than other people."

"Yes, *better off* even though they are so bad. I'll tell you why, Fluffy. They've got the Faith, though they don't keep to what it tells them, and so if they get frightened and sorry for their sins they know what they've got to do, and that there's only one thing in the world that can set them right."

"I see," said Fluffy thoughtfully; "them that's *not* Catholics and begin to feel frightened at their sins, why they're all took of a heap, as one may say, and don't know what to be at. If they goes to the parson, he tells 'em to b'lieve, and that don't seem no help. I knows that."

"But Father Dunstan told you more than that, I'm sure, Fluffy."

"Yes, I'm a-gettin' on," said Fluffy. "He's been a-goin' at me to-day about sin— Adam and Eve's sin. He says I've never got free of a stain it made on me, if I've never been baptised."

"And you haven't?"

"No, I'm pretty certain I hasn't.
Leastways I never heard tell of it. That
*do* seem strange how some water poured
over me can take off the sins as Adam and
Eve did."

"You've got to believe it though," said
Charlie stoutly. "Our religion tells us
what's true, and don't expect us to ask a
lot of questions, and say we can't understand."

"So it seems," said Fluffy; and having
reached the church, they went in, one boy
to make his way to the sacristy, the other to
kneel at the bottom of the church with eyes
fixed intently on the door from which he
knew Charlie would presently enter.

He came at last with the other boys and
Father Dunstan, and the poor untaught lad
listened to the hymn which was sung, and
listened still more to the sermon which

followed, in which he now and then caught some words he could understand.

But it was when the Benediction service commenced—when light and incense, and the voice of men, women, and children joined in praising the Lord of heaven and earth, that Fluffy's eyes brightened and his face was eager and admiring. The priest had told him that Jesus—the thorn-crowned crucified Saviour, the Friend Who had always loved and always watched him—was there. Within that little door, now opened, Fluffy knew that Jesus lived always; but never till then had he *felt* that presence, felt the love which stole into his heart and won it from sin.

" Lord, I believe "—no, he did not say the words, for he had never heard them; but that was what his heart said, although from his lips came only in a half-whisper,

" I'll do it, Lord Jesus Christ ; I won't hold
out no longer."

When Fluffy went in the early morning to
the priest's house, he waited impatiently for
Father Dunstan to finish his Mass—then he
sought him.

" Father !" and the boy's voice showed in
some measure the earnestness of his heart,
" You'd best make me a Catholic. I've
thought about it, and I'm going to believe it
all, and I'll try and do it too. Jesus and
Mary shan't wait for me no longer."

That day Fluffy was baptised. At night
he told the good news to his friend, Mrs.
Murphy.

" I'm not Fluffy no more," he said. " I
don't mind being called it, if it comes easier
to all of you, mum ; but I've got a real good
name of my own now—I'm John Dunstan."

# CHAPTER XI.

"Now, John," said Father Dunstan, the day after Fluffy's baptism, "I want to tell you about the saints whose names you have received. Do you know what I mean when I speak of *saints?*"

"Well—they're good, I s'pose," was the reply, after a few moments' reflection.

"Yes, very good. So good that we can only hope to be a little like them; yet we must try, and we must pray. They are happy and glorious in the presence of God, and yet they watch over us, and help us by their prayers."

"Can they see all that way off?" said

Fluffy, looking doubtful—for "Fluffy" we must still call him.

"Yes. Though they are in heaven and we are on earth, they know what is happening to us, and when we are in trouble or in temptation they will pray to God for us if we ask them."

There was a pause, but as Fluffy asked no question nor showed signs of any doubt, Father Dunstan went on:

"There have been many saints whose name was John; but the one of whom I was especially thinking when I called you by that name is Saint John the Evangelist. He is then your 'patron saint,' which means that you are placed in a special way under his care or patronage."

Fluffy nodded his head, as a sign that he comprehended very well what was being said to him.

" I shall give you a picture of Saint John to keep, so that when you look at it, you may remember he was very dear to Christ, so dear that he was allowed to lean his head upon the Sacred Heart of our Lord; and he is called the 'beloved disciple'—beloved because of his purity of heart."

"What were the end of him?" said Fluffy.

"He died when he was quite old—the only one of Christ's apostles who was not put to death. But he had suffered a great deal which I will tell you some other time when I think you can understand better. Just now I want you to think that Saint John, who was so pure, and so good, and whose heart was full of love to Jesus, is watching over you. If you pray to him, he will ask God to give you grace also to be good and pure."

"And what about t'other one?" said Fluffy, somewhat abruptly.

"You mean Saint Dunstan—try always to speak respectfully of the saints. Well, this holy man was born many, many hundred years ago, and was taught by some good priests whom we call monks. He had been specially given to the Blessed Mother of God at his birth, and she watched over him, and obtained for him great graces from Heaven. Dunstan became very clever, and he could make brass and other metal ornaments for the church. While he worked, he turned his thoughts to God and tried to labour well just as if our Lord was standing by his side. Now and then the devil came and tried to put evil into his mind, but Saint Dunstan would not listen, and drove the devil away. I want you to think very much of Saint Dunstan when *you* get to work, my boy. I dare say you will feel the devil putting bad thoughts into your heart, trying to make you dishonest or untruthful, perhaps. At such times you must call Saint Dunstan to help you, and remember that *he* would not listen to the devil, neither must you."

"I see," said Fluffy. "But then I haven't got any work to do, except what turns up here."

"But that little you can do well. No 'scamping' it, you know, but thoroughly, as you would if you could see our Lord looking on, pleased and glad when you do the least thing faithfully."

Fluffy looked at the priest for an instant, and then, casting his eyes on his boots, seemed very much confused.

"You want to say something—to ask something, perhaps," said Father Dunstan.

" Out with it ; surely you are not afraid ?"

" No—that is, not exactly," and Fluffy stammered and coloured more than ever. "I hope as I'm not ungrateful to you, Father, for keeping me on here, but I'd be glad if I could find a reg'lar place. I'd like to get in a shop if I could."

The priest smiled. " I know all about it, Fluffy, and I have not been idle. The reason I told you to-day about your patron saints was because I think you will want their help very much just now. There is a place found for you, if you try to please and to be a good boy."

Fluffy's face brightened at that.

" Johnson, the grocer at the corner of the next street, wants a boy, and he has promised me to give you a trial. Now how do you mean to behave yourself?"

" Fust-rate," responded Fluffy, promptly.

"I would rather hear you say, 'I will try,'" remarked Father Dunstan. "If you think it an easy matter which you can manage by yourself, I know very well that you will fall back into sin. You are certain to be tempted, my lad. The devil will try and make you think there is no harm in helping yourself to your master's goods, perhaps; then he may get you to tell a lie to hide what you have done, and then will follow more dishonesty and more lies until you fall into some great sin which will be found out, and your character will be gone."

Fluffy looked somewhat startled at such a picture; then, recovering himself, he said, "If I came to confession and told it all, you could get me right again."

"Yes, I could give you God's pardon for all your sins if you were very sorry and resolved to give them up. But you must also determine first of all not to do wrong. You must promise me to ask Jesus and Mary and your patron saints to keep you safe, and try, too, very hard yourself, or else you cannot go on Monday morning to Mr. Johnson's."

Fluffy still wore a doubtful look. "It's a grocer, didn't you say, Father?"

"Yes, you must pass the door as you go from here to Mrs. Murphy's."

"Yes, I knows," said Fluffy. "It isn't what one might call a big shop, but there's raisins and currants and such-like things in the winder—and sweets too."

"And you are fond of sweets and raisins and currants?" asked the priest, watching the boy's face.

"I b'lieve you," said Fluffy, with some enthusiasm. "I'm certain to get a-tasting of 'em if I'm there. P'raps I'd best give it up."

" Because you will be tempted? That is not right, Fluffy. Only think of the change which has come over you. Not very long since you were a poor ignorant boy who did not know even that Christ died for you. Now, you have heard of Him, you have become a member of His own Church, His Blood has washed away the stains of your old bad life from your soul—with all this grace can't you fight against a little temptation for Christ's sake ?"

Still Fluffy hesitated. " P'raps somethin' in the greengrocery line 'd suit me better; but then there's certain to be apples, to say nothin' of pears ! It seems to me as if the devil 'd be in every shop I'd get into."

" Then you do not wish to go to Mr. Johnson's for a trial ?"

" Yes, I do," said Fluffy. " Don't you see, Father, how it is ? I'd like to go, and

yet I b'lieves as it's not in me to keep clear
of them raisins and things."

"No, it is not in *you*, but God can help
you, and He will. Go and do your best,
Fluffy, and as long as you are afraid to
trust yourself and pray hard to be kept from
sin, I do not fear for you."

The matter being thus settled, Fluffy's
spirits rose every hour, and he could scarcely
wait till evening to tell his news to his friend
Mrs. Murphy. Being sent on an errand or
two by Father Dunstan's housekeeper, he was
desperately tempted to run round that way,
and paused at a street-corner to decide
whether he should venture.

"It'd be precious awkward if I come across
Father Dunstan, and there's no knowin'
where he may be," thus he argued with himself. "And then, he said only this mornin'
as the Lord Jesus were a-lookin' just as if I

see Him close by. No, I'll wait till night, my news'll keep, and I shouldn't like any one to see me a-cuttin' the other way when I ought to be back from my errands."

It was a victory, although a small one; and Fluffy felt almost for the first time, the happiness which we all experience when we have overcome a temptation.

"I *am* glad, that I am!" so said Mrs. Murphy when she heard the news about Johnson, the grocer; and Charlie and his father too seemed to share in Fluffy's delight.

"I don't know whether it's true," said Murphy, with a funny twinkle in his eyes, as he turned them towards the boy; "I don't know, but I've *heard* that when a grocer gets a new lad, he just lets him have the run of all that's in the shop, currants and figs and the like. In one week he's had enough of it—a downright sickener, as the saying is, and he never wants to bo tasting them again."

Fluffy's face had beamed when Mr. Murphy first spoke, but it wore a very grave look when all was said.

" I'm afeard it wouldn't be a sickener for *me*," he said, with a sigh.  "I don't believe as six weeks'd tire me so as I wouldn't want to taste no more. . That's just what I'm afeard of—not bein' able to keep from them sort of good things.  It's bad enough even to pass the winder."

"Oh yes, you can, if you say a 'Hail, Mary,'" said Mrs. Murphy encouragingly. "That's what I do when I want help, and you do the same;" and then she went on speaking brightly of Fluffy's future, drawing a charming picture of a time when by God's blessing, added to honesty and hard work, he might be master of a shop as good as Johnson's.

The boy listened, but he did not seem to care very much for such a prospect. "It couldn't ever come true for such as me," he said. "I *knows* as it couldn't come true, and yet I often thinks what I would be when I'm a man if I had my choice."

"And what is that?" said Mrs. Murphy, while Charlie echoed the question.

Fluffy hesitated. Evidently the wish to tell was overpowered by the fear of being laughed at.

"I *know* it can't come true," he said again, growing very red. "I'm not a scholard, nor never shall be; for a poor lad like me must get his livin', instead of going to school; but if I *were* a scholard, I'd like—"

"To be a priest," interrupted Charlie, and if the truth be told, there was some scorn in his tone. "I know you've heard some of the fellows in the sacristy say it, so you say it too."

"I haven't," cried Fluffy, angry now. "I don't know what they say, for I've never been there but that once, and I don't care neither. I never *thought* of bein' a priest; it'd be a fine thing for such as me to get into my head, wouldn't it?"

"Come, Charlie, you have nothing to do with it," said Mrs. Murphy, at the same time giving her son a look which he well understood to mean disapproval. "Tell me your wish, if you don't mind, Fluffy. You know I like to hear all that you care for."

Her quiet way soothed the anger of the boy's heart.

"'Tisn't such a great thing," he said. "It's only great for such as me. I'd have liked to learn myself, so as when I'm a man

I could teach. I'd like to be the master in a school where the boys was very poor and rough—same as me. I think I'd know how to give 'em a kind of a lift when they was all down and all wrong—you see I knows what it is by myself."

"I call it a very good wish," said Mrs. Murphy seriously. "I don't myself see how it can come to pass ; still, more unlikely things have happened."

"Of course they have," struck in Mr. Murphy. "If poor little Dick Whittington had told any one he wanted to be Lord Mayor of London they would have laughed at him, yet he was."

"I never heard tell of him," said Fluffy, growing interested. "He wasn't so poor and low as me, I s'pose."

"He was as poor as he could well be," said Mr. Murphy. "His father and his mother were dead, and there wasn't a friend in all the world to help him, so he thought he'd leave his native village and come up to London."

"What for?" said Fluffy.

"To seek his fortune. Countryfolk seem to think always that money's to be had almost for the picking up, once they get to London, and it seems that Dick Whittington thought so too. But after a day or two's tramping, he began to get downhearted, and at last he sat himself down by the road-side, wishing he had never left his native village, wishing almost that he was dead."

"Poor little chap," said Fluffy.

"Well, but listen to the end. As he sat there—away at Highgate it was—he could see the spires of the churches and the distant houses in the great city, and all of a sudden the bells came ringing out merrily—

ringing so loudly that little Dick heard them
there by the wayside on Highgate Hill. I
suppose he was a fanciful boy, and being
tired and faint, he got dreamy, and began to
think the bells rang out words. And then
it seemed to him that he understood what
the words were : 'Turn again, Whittington,
Lord Mayor of London.' Though it
was only a fancy, it put new heart
into the little chap. No more thinking of
going back to his native village for Dick !
He got up, and shouldered his bundle, and
marched on to London, and when he got
there he turned into a shop, and asked the
master to take him."

"And did he ?" cried Fluffy.

" Ay, that he did, and Dick got on from
one thing to another until he was a rich
man—so rich that he built some of the
great places we've got in the city. Now,

Fluffy, if you want to know how, I can only tell you it was by being upright and hard-working." And here Mr. Murphy brought his story to a close, rather surprised at himself for being betrayed into so much talking, for he was a man of few words.

"I like that story," said Fluffy. "I wish the bells would bring me a message."

"That was all Dick's fancy, you know," put in Mrs. Murphy. "But it helped him on. I'd have a fancy, if I were you, Fluffy. Whenever you hear our church-bell ringing, just you think it says, 'Learn away, John Dunstan—you'll be a schoolmaster.'"

They all laughed at that, but Fluffy soon grew serious as he said, "It's no use a-tellin' me to learn away; I can't learn myself, and I've no one to learn me."

"I dare say I could help you a bit of evenings if you like," said Charlie, speaking at last. Poor Charlie had been wrestling with his enemy during his father's story, and had only just got the best of it.

"You don't mean it?" said Fluffy.

"Yes, I do. Why shouldn't I?"

"Oh, I don't know; only it'd be a deal of bother; but there, I don't know if I'll get any evenings. Father Dunstan didn't say a word about hours, but I'm to go to Mr. Johnson to-morrow, and then I'll hear all I can."

"Yes, do," said Mrs. Murphy. "Charlie will help you get on with your reading and writing, I know. We'll see about it when once you find out what time you'll have for yourself, Fluffy."

## CHAPTER XII.

Poor Fluffy returned to his friends somewhat out of spirits next evening.

They beset him with questions, but did
not light upon the cause of his depression.

He had got the place? oh yes, Mr.
Johnson was quite willing to give him a trial.
He liked his master?—yes, he had nothing
to say against him. It was not until supper
was set upon the table that Fluffy's spirits
entirely gave way and the truth came out.
He was to sleep at the grocer's shop, so
there was an end of any plan for learning
from Charlie; an end, too, to the happy
evenings in that comfortable little house. .

Although he knew that Mrs. Murphy took him in at Father Dunstan's request, although he had known too it could not go on so always, his little makeshift bed had become very dear and familiar to him, and it was hard to leave it.

"We shall miss you dreadfully, Fluffy," said Mrs. Murphy kindly. "You've grown to seem just like one of us. I don't mean to give you up even if you *are* going away. I'm going to see to your things just exactly as I do for Charlie, and you must try and feel as if I were a sort of mother to you— will you?"

Fluffy's answer was a low, deep sob; but no one there thought him ungrateful.

"You must come and spend Sundays here," she went on kindly. "Your master can't want you then, and we will all go to Mass together and have a nice long day, and get

Benediction in the evening. Why, we shall be looking forward to Sunday all the week through !"

Fluffy gave a very watery kind of smile, but Mrs. Murphy had set her mind upon showing him the bright side of things.

" It will seem just as if I had another boy of my own—Patrick or little Tom, who died long ago—to have you coming home every week telling me all that's happened. For remember you've got a home here as long as you want one, Fluffy, and there's a welcome always ready and waiting for you."

Another sob, though the boy was struggling hard not to cry ; but then kindness always touched Fluffy's heart, it was even yet so new to him.

" Well, then for the learning," said Mrs. Murphy ; " I can't see why you shouldn't practise your reading and your writing too,

12—2

perhaps. Charlie can find books for you, and surely you'll have a few minutes to yourself now and again. On Sundays you could go over it together, and you will get on that way, if it is but slowly—at any rate it will be better than nothing."

Fluffy cheered up a little at this; but once alone, and lying in his snug bed, he cried bitterly and long. Only three nights and he would be away from the place which had first given him any idea of a home.

When Monday morning came, Fluffy presented himself at the appointed hour at Mr. Johnson's shop, and when he had said good-bye to the Murphys he did not feel so very sad—the mere thought that he was going to make his first start in a respectable way of earning a living was pleasant.

" I wonder how that Dick what's-his-name felt when he turned into a shop and

asked for to be took," he thought to himself; " I expect he had one or two turns
afore the door till he'd got the pluck to go
in—I know *I* should;" and Fluffy went on a
few yards past the grocer's door, glad to
know the clocks had not yet struck eight,
and therefore he had still some moments
of freedom remaining.

However, they were but few, and with a
beating heart the boy presented himself
before his new master. He looked a bright,
tidy little chap now—the Dockett's-buildings people would have passed him by, I
think, as a stranger. Regular food had
worked wonders in his appearance, considering it was but a fortnight since he had
fallen into kind hands. Soap and water
had done much, and besides, was he not
clothed in one of Charlie Murphy's out-
grown suits? a suit as tidy and good as any

boy of the working-class could wish to put on. The consciousness of being respectably dressed, the intercourse with respectable people, had already rubbed off some of Fluffy's extreme roughness. He left off sundry expressions which had done very well for the streets, but which he felt out of keeping with his new circumstances; he would listen as Charlie talked with his father and mother, trying to catch their way and to give up his own style of expressing himself. It was slow work to do this, but even now any one who noticed would have seen the difference between the Fluffy of the present, and Fluffy of a fortnight earlier—a difference which became more marked every day.

" To think that all this is work I might have done long ago, and never gave a thought to!" Mrs. Murphy would say to her husband as she sat stitching or mending for

Fluffy through the long evenings. "Many
and many a poor boy I might have helped
and never missed the little it cost me;
but there—I never seemed to see before that
it was any but the rich folk's business!"

"It runs through us all, I'm thinking," so
Murphy would answer. "We can all busy
ourselves with finding out what other folks can
do and ought to do, and what we *would* do if
we was them, and so we let the time go and
let the work go too, which Our Blessed Lord is
looking to get from us—God forgive us all."

Charlie, too, used to think a good deal
when he heard his father and mother talking
thus. He had made up his mind to befriend
Fluffy, and already Denis Smith and his
other friends were growing tired of joking
and teasing him about it; still, he never
now met a dirty hungry-looking child in
the street without thinking it *might* be

another Fluffy, and instead of passing on
unconcernedly as once he would have done,
many a penny which would otherwise have
gone in sweets, found its way into some
baker's shop to bring a roll or a bun to the
hands of the street boy or girl.

Charlie used to build up great schemes
for doing good to the very poor when he
was a man too. *He* had his schemes and
purposes like every other boy, and though
he did not feel any wish to be a priest, as
his parents would have perhaps desired to
see, he meant to serve God well in the
world, and get on as far as God would let
him. *Supposing* he was able to get into
some merchant's office when he left school,
oh how he meant to try to advance from
one step to another ! and so when he was a
man, father should work no more, and mother
should have an easy life in her old age, and

some neat little maid to do the house-work
for her. That was the height of Charlie
Murphy's ambition, and it was a purpose he
intended to achieve if work and care availed
anything. And then he had one very
firmly-rooted belief too, one which we would
gladly see in all boys—he believed that as
long as he kept close to God, kept faithful
to his religious duties, even worldly projects
were likely to be successful ; while to forget
God and neglect his religion, would be to
lose this world and the next also.

Truly Charlie knew that now and then,
Godless men and women appear to prosper ;
but then he also knew that such prosperity
was never lasting, never happy, and Charlie
was too true a Catholic to want any good
fortune of *that* kind—stronger even than
his wish to advance himself was the wish to
be true to God and the faith.

And yet with all this good-will he was not a perfect boy. He had all the natural faults of many boys, a hot temper—this good opinion of himself which we have seen him discover—and a host more imperfections. But there was nothing mean or untruthful about young Murphy, and with his steady purpose to do right, there was every reason to believe he would one day be wholly master of himself.

The first week of Fluffy's absence seemed long to every one. Father Dunstan had made a point of going into the shop to see for himself how the boy was going on. Mrs. Murphy was always finding out some business which took her that way so that she might catch, perhaps, a glimpse of Fluffy's face and cheer him by one of her bright smiles, while Charlie invested several times in sweets on purpose to report concerning his young friend. Upon the last of those occasions Fluffy served him, and I could never describe to you the experienced air with which he weighed the sweets and made them into a parcel—it sent Charlie into an irrepressible fit of laughter which the young shopman rather resented.

"Come now, what are you a-laughing at?" he inquired, for it was early, and just then neither Mr. Johnson nor any customers were in the shop.

"I can't help it, you do think yourself so precious big," and Charlie chuckled again; then, seeing Fluffy's heightened colour, he added, "You do it uncommonly well, I must say though. I shall tell mother to come and get some tea here, and mind you serve her."

"Oh, I can't," said Fluffy; "if master isn't in the shop I have to call him, except it's for sweets. There's such a lot of little brats coming for a farthing's worth of sweets that he leaves me to serve them."

"And how many have you eaten?" said Charlie.

Fluffy hesitated. " I haven't *taken* any. I can't say as when one or two is left over weight I always puts them back. Somehow it comes natural to taste them and see what kind of stuff I've been selling, but I haven't done it on the sly, and the master don't say nothing. I say, Charlie, though! you tell your father that's all a take-in about boys having leave to eat what they like the first week. *I* haven't had no such leave, still now and then they've give me a fig or two. Mrs. Johnson's the best for that."

"And so you're getting on tolerably well ?" said Charlie, feeling his time was short, and he must not prolong the conversation.

"Oh yes, pretty middlin'," said Fluffy. "I'll tell you all about it Sunday; I'm a-coming round as soon as I'm up, and I needn't get in till nine in the evening. I say, Charlie, if you come here, and I'm not in, or busy with another customer, don't you ever buy any sweets out of that bottle there. The missis give me some one day, and they ain't half so good as Parker's—them raspberry-drops, I mean. Now the 'cidulated, or them toffee-drops, I can recommend, for I've tried 'em both."

"All right," laughed Charlie. "It won't please Mr. Johnson, though, if you warn people not to buy his things, but go to Parker's. Good-bye, Fluffy, I shall be late for school if I stop another minute." And away he went, thinking what fun it would be to describe the interview to his father and mother at dinner-time.

It was scarcely light on Sunday morning when Fluffy presented himself at Mrs. Murphy's door. He glanced at the windows before he knocked, but no one seemed stirring.

"Not up!" he exclaimed. "Well, if they ain't, they ought to be; so here goes," and he applied himself to the knocker.

"Who upon earth is that?" cried Mrs. Murphy, opening her eyes. "If it wasn't Sunday, I should say it was the sweep, for I've ordered him to come at six to-morrow. Dear! dear! how they do knock, and I can't get my things on any quicker; no, not if my sister in Bermondsey is taken ill or dying."

"We've overslept ourselves," said Murphy, looking at his big silver watch, the best timekeeper in all England, he was wont to say. "It's past seven o'clock, and we were going to the eight o'clock Mass. So we can now, if we look sharp. Don't hurry yourself to get to the door; there's Charlie going down."

Mrs. Murphy being by this time ready to present herself, went out and leaned over the stairs to catch the message ; surely her sister or one of the children must be ill, and she was wanted immediately !

But Fluffy's familiar vòice reached her ears, and she went back to her husband, laughing.

"Why, it's Fluffy," she said. "I told him to come as early as he could, and yet I never once gave it a thought that it could be him at this time. I'll light the fire, and put on the kettle, and make everything ready for breakfast as soon as we get in. We are in time for the eight Mass now, thanks to Fluffy. If it hadn't been for him we might have slept on another hour, so I'm glad he came."

There was a warm greeting between them ; to Mrs. Murphy the poor, friendless boy was becoming almost like a child of her own.

" We are going to early Mass, Fluffy," she said. " Then we'll get a nice long day. It's Charlie's Communion Sunday, too. Ah ! how glad we'll be when we see you going to receive Our Blessed Lord. When is that going to be, Fluffy ?"

The boy looked down shyly ; even to her —his good, kind friend—he could not say how he thought of such a happiness, how he longed for it, too, and yet how he feared that even now he could never be half good enough for Jesus, the pure and Holy God, to come into his heart.

Fluffy had not yet understood that it is

not possible for him or any one to be fit to receive so great a guest, only that He accepts our will, our desire, and pitying our weakness, comes to fill our hearts with His purity, His humility, His holiness—not our own.

## CHAPTER XIII.

WHEN Charlie came to inquire into Fluffy's progress in study, he found it but small.

There had not been many spare moments during the day, and when the shop was shut the boy was expected to get his supper and be off to bed. Still, he had managed to spell out a few pages in the reading-book, so that he could make out the meaning of the words, and go over it all a little more fluently with Charlie to assist him.

On Sunday morning, after Mass and breakfast, Fluffy wrote his first copy; a smeary spluttery page of strokes, certainly, when finished, but still it *was* a "copy," and the young writer looked at his performance with great satisfaction.

"It isn't as good as I could wish," he said, as he sucked the tips of his inky fingers. "All the same I never'd have thought I could do it as well." And no one discouraged him by speaking of the deficiencies.

"You ought to learn a bit of Catechism every Sunday," said Charlie, when the reading and writing were concluded.

Fluffy looked disconsolate. "Won't it do as well if you tell me what's in it?" he said. "Father Dunstan, he began when I was there—he told me all about God making me, and how I'd got to do what the Church teaches us, and believe it too. I didn't get it by heart."

"No, because Father Dunstan wanted you to understand certain things before you

13—2

were baptised. Catholics always learn their Catechism if they can read at all."

"Oh, well if I must, why I must," said Fluffy. "Here, give us hold," and taking the little green book he glanced down the first page.

"I've got to say that—word for word?"

Charlie nodded. "You ought, Fluffy," he said, hardly knowing whether it were well to insist on the point, and yet unwilling to let his pupil off what he deemed a very necessary study.

Fluffy took the book over to the fire, and no one could get a word from him till just before dinner, when he announced his ability to say the first few answers of the Catechism. He acquitted himself so well that he was quite pleased, and from that time his lessons in Christian doctrine were regularly established, to Charlie Murphy's great satisfaction.

The second week at the grocer's shop passed off well, and Fluffy, growing more accustomed to his duties, made himself so useful that at the month's end Mr. Johnson declared himself quite satisfied, and willing to keep him as long as he continued to behave well.

It was a proud and happy moment for Fluffy when he could tell the priest that he was to have the place, for his month's trial had been satisfactory, and his eyes shone with delight as Father Dunstan spoke a few kind words of approval.

Proud and happy also was Fluffy when his prospects were talked over on the Sunday at the Murphys. In his own way he seemed to understand that by his good conduct he could prove himself grateful to those who had helped him when he was friendless.

" And how about the raisins and things?"

said Mrs. Murphy. "Do they tempt you dreadfully?"

Fluffy nodded. "I b'lieve you. The first week I used to eat any that got out loose on the counter, or if there was a few sweets over-weight they'd go into my mouth. But Father Dunstan stopped that. He said it was a sort of playing with temptation, and if he was me he'd make a rule never to eat one that wasn't give to me. I've kept to it too, only I couldn't unless I'd said a Hail Mary, as you told me, when I felt tempted uncommonly."

"Ah, you do what Father Dunstan tells you, my lad, and you'll grow up a good and honest man. And if you get to be a schoolmaster, Fluffy, you'll be able to tell your boys how to be good, and help them too, all the better because you've had to try hard yourself."

"Oh, I dare say!" exclaimed Fluffy, look-ing, however, highly delighted. "It's fine to talk of me being a schoolmaster."

"Don't forget Dick Whittington," said Mr. Murphy; "and not only him, but many more boys have risen up from being poor to be wise and great."

"I don't want to be great," said Fluffy. "It isn't great to be master at a school of poor boys. What are you going to be, Charlie?"

"Oh, I don't know," said the other hurriedly—it was not his way to tell out all those bright visions he spun by the fireside when he was supposed to be reading—but thinking it might seem ungracious he added, "I'd like to be a clerk in the City, and I mean to be too, if I can."

"Well, so long as you both fear God and keep His commandments, it does not greatly matter what you are," said Mrs. Murphy, trying to smother a little regret which always came when she found Charlie's taste was not exactly like her own would have been for him.

Nothing very eventful happened in Fluffy's life during the months of spring and early summer, but a great change was gradually passing over him, not only in outward appearance, but in his thoughts and feelings.

He was not a rough boy now. The old vulgar expressions were forgotten or laid aside, his speech was as good as Charlie Murphy's own, his manners even quieter, but all this was little compared to the altered state of his heart.

Perhaps that deep, hidden longing for his first Communion was doing a work of its own; perhaps it was the desire to fit himself to receive so infinite a blessing that made him love to pray, and love to make those secret visits to the Blessed Sacrament, which no one knew but God. Had he an errand lying in the direction of the church, Fluffy felt that one moment of prayer in the dear presence of Jesus helped him all day long and was no waste of time, for his feet went all the more quickly and readily after. Even if the door was closed, the prayer went up from his heart as he passed on, and that prayer was always, " Lord Jesus, get me ready to receive Thee into my heart. Teach me to love Thee and to hate sin."

Fluffy would have told you that in no other way could he have resisted the temptations of the grocer's shop—Jesus would never want to come to a boy who pilfered from his master !

He used to think a great deal at this time of his mother. Oh ! if only she had known what it was to be a Catholic, if only she had

had a priest to tell her how to save her soul !
As it was, Fluffy did not know whether
she had ever heard of One Who died for
her. He thought, too, of the people in
Dockett's-buildings, of the sinful lives they
led, and a great sorrow filled his heart.
Had he been a man, I think nothing would
have kept Fluffy from finding his way there
to tell them what he had learned himself ;
being a boy, he could only pray to his
Mother Mary for them, and pray that he
might be forgiven for all he had done evil
while he lived among them.

Thus thinking, thus praying, and thus
striving to do right, Fluffy passed the spring-
time of that first year of his new life ; when
summer came the quick eyes of Mrs. Murphy
noted weakness in the boy's movements, a
pallor of face, and an unnatural heaviness
about his eyes which troubled her.

She questioned him, but no complaint
came. He was "very well, always well,
only sometimes tired," he said.

Another week or two, and then in the
heat of a midsummer day Fluffy came home,
as Mrs. Murphy had bidden him come if anything was the matter. His master had seen
he was ill, and sent him to take a rest till
the next morning.

But when morning came there was no
getting up for Fluffy. Tossing feverishly in
his little bed he talked of his mother, of
Dockett's-buildings, even of the prison days
and Joe Rogers ; but he did not recognise
the kind face bent anxiously over him.

"Fever"—that was the doctor's decision
when he was sent for ; "the boy had better
go to the hospital," he said ; "for it was
impossible as yet to say how severe it would
be."

But Mrs. Murphy resisted that idea. It was Fluffy's home, and at home he should stay. It was not likely that she would take the infection, if such there was, and she should nurse him as if he was her own boy. As for Charlie—well, Mary the Mother of Mercy would watch over him and over them all, and they would pray to Saint Roche to keep contagion from them.

But Fluffy's illness proved to be some tedious low fever which wanted care and patient watching, and he had both; Mrs. Murphy rarely left him either by day or night, and when she did her husband or Charlie took her place.

After a time it was said that Fluffy was getting better, and yet he seemed so weak that Father Dunstan grew very anxious about him.

"My dear boy," he said one warm July

evening, when he had been sitting some time in the sick-room, "the doctor says you will recover, but we never can be quite sure what God may choose for us. Suppose He meant to take you away from this world, are you willing to die ?"

Fluffy's lip quivered. " I don't know, Father," he said hesitatingly. "There's something lonesome and strange in dying— it seemed so when mother went. I dare say it's the best thing for me though. Perhaps if I lived to be a man, I couldn't keep right and straight—I'd rather die now than think of that."

" Yes, indeed—better far for God to take you in your youth than for you to turn away from Him when He has been so very, very good to you. Do you try and think how good He has been ?"

" I'm always thinking of it, Father," said

Fluffy simply. "When I lie awake at night I keep wondering how I'd have managed if I had been ill in those days when there was nowhere to call home. And then it seems to come before me that God has been taking care of me all through, even when I was so wicked. If I had lived I'd have liked to do something for Him to show Him I'm grateful, but I don't know—perhaps I never could."

" We will leave that to God," said Father Dunstan. "Only try to resolve that living or dying, you will be all His. But there is something more I want to say to you before I go. Do you never feel a wish to receive our Blessed Lord into your heart, my boy ? You know what this means, for you have learned what the Catechism teaches. You know that Jesus, the King of heaven and earth, humbles Himself to come to us sinful creatures that He may bless and make us good. Did you never wish Him to come to you ?"

The expression of face, the nervous clasping of the thin hands, was sufficient answer even if Fluffy had not spoken. " Oh Father," and his voice trembled, " I don't think I ever could tell you how much I've wished it ! There are times when it seemed as if I couldn't keep from crying when other boys went to Communion and never me. I've even fancied sometimes how He would look with His beautiful kind face and His hands held up to bless everybody as He says, ' Come unto Me.' I've thought all that till it seemed so real I almost could think I heard Him say the words, and yet—-and yet—" and Fluffy broke into an agony of tears.

" Oh, my dear boy, why did you never tell me—never let me know you had these

thoughts and wishes ?" said Father Dunstan,
whose own eyes glistened at Fluffy's simple
tale.

"I didn't dare," said the boy in a
whisper. "Times and times again I thought
I would, and then I remembered all I'd
been and all the terrible evil of my life.   It
seemed as if I had been so bad, it must take
years and years to make me ready.   I think
it has helped me to keep on trying though,"
he added.

"I shall let you make your first Communion here on your sick-bed," said Father
Dunstan.   "If it is God's Will to raise you
up, the coming of His dear Son will give
you strength.   If He chooses death for you,
you will not feel lonely any more—our Lord
will be with you through the dark valley."

"Yes, I'd not be afraid then," said Fluffy,
smiling.

"Well, now, for the next three days we will pray very much, and talk together of Jesus in the Blessed Sacrament, and then He will come to you my boy, never, never to be cast out of your heart again, except by wilful sin."

"Oh, please, Father, shall I be ready?" said Fluffy earnestly. "It seems such a great thing for Him to come to me."

"Yes, but it is what He longs to do, Fluffy. He knows you are weak and easily tempted, so He wants to give you His own strength. He is coming to help you to live or to help you to die, and you need not fear Him. You know Who He is, you long for Him, you are sorry for all your sins; and this merciful, tender Saviour asks no more."

So three days after, Fluffy received his God—so fervently, so lovingly, that Mrs.

14

Murphy thought it must be God's way of making him ready to die; but Father Dunstan thought otherwise. It seemed given him to see then that the coming of Jesus was to bring life, not death, to the sick boy; and he was right, for Fluffy grew stronger from that hour.

## CHAPTER XIV.

On one of the days when Fluffy was getting better, Charlie Murphy came in with "news to tell" clearly written on his face.

"Here's a go, Fluffy," he said. "Johnson has taken another boy in your place; he can't wait any longer, he says."

Charlie never thought what the effect might be of such tidings; he scarcely even noticed the whiteness which overspread Fluffy's already pale face, and for a few moments he went on speaking of the new boy who had been taken into Mr. Johnson's employ. Suddenly, he saw a glitter in

Fluffy's eyes which looked suspiciously like tears.

"You're crying about it," he exclaimed. "Don't do that, Fluffy. There are places enough besides his, never you fear."

"Yes, I know," said Fluffy, trying hard not to cry. "There's places enough, but not the sort for me. I'm not like you; I'm not up to anything much. Oh, Charlie, if only I'd learned when I was little."

"You'll do all right," said Charlie good-naturedly, although he scarcely knew how the "righting" process was to be brought about. "You can read a little, you know."

"Yes, but it's a poor sort of reading," said Fluffy. "I'd give anything if I could go to school."

The two boys were talking over the difficulty when the priest came in, and

Charlie soon made him acquainted with Fluffy's desires.

"Well, I think I have good news for you," he said. "First of all, I have a situation for you. It is only at a small greengrocer's shop, but the woman is a good Catholic body, and she will let you out to the night school three evenings in the week."

Fluffy's face brightened, but then, remembering the pears, apples, nuts, and other temptations which would come in his way, he sighed.

"I will tell you something to help you," said Father Dunstan, when he found what the boy was thinking of. "There was a great servant and apostle of Christ, whom we know as Saint Paul. Though he was so holy, God allowed him to be tempted, and *so much* tempted that Saint Paul prayed that he might be delivered from it. What do you think was God's answer? He did not send away the temptation; He only reminded the Apostle that he had not to strive against it alone. 'My grace is sufficient for thee,' He said, and with that grace Saint Paul beat down the tempter beneath his feet, just as you and I too can do by the same grace of God."

It seemed to help Fluffy already.

"I'll try, Father," he said; and try he did, too, when the time came for him to enter upon his new duties.

Mrs. Brian—Fluffy's employer—was a good old body, but being old she was often cross, and the boy found it hard to bear. She had one idea firmly fixed in her mind, and it was this: a boy was a necessary evil in her shop—but still an evil; something to be watched, and questioned, and scolded; a being who would be always playing at

street corners or idling away his time unless
she "kept her eye upon him," as she said.

I dare say Mrs. Brian would have done anything for Fluffy's good, either of body or soul ;
what she could not do, was to remember
he was only a boy, and so be patient.

And as Fluffy grew strong and well again,
I must confess he needed patience, for he
was full of tricks—full sometimes of sharp,
saucy answers. He did not mean any
harm, nor did he fall away from God at this
time. I suppose he did not see just then
that smaller faults must be corrected as
well as greater.

Mrs. Murphy, catching him playing
chuckpenny one day with a party of
crossing-sweepers, was grievously distressed
about Fluffy, and went straight to Father
Dunstan to say that being at Mrs. Brian's
shop would be the ruin of him.

On being questioned, Fluffy owned to indulging in chuckpenny at times when his duty called him elsewhere, but he told of the pleasure of the game and the delight of escaping Mrs. Brian's vigilance so candidly that the priest felt quite sure, whatever were his faults, there was nothing hidden. Oh, had he but been able to put this poor lad into some good school away from the streets and the temptations of a young shop-boy, how gladly he would have done so, but he could not. Hundreds more such boys were all around; hundreds of men, women, and children, all needing help, all asking help far greater than he could give. Father Dunstan could only watch over Fluffy, and pray for him.

But fortune, far better than any of his friends had ever imagined for him, was coming. An old lady, attending the church and living in the neighbourhood, noticed Fluffy, and hearing something of his history, asked more. When she was told how he longed to go to school, she said his wish should be granted; to school he must be sent, and at her expense.

When Fluffy heard this news, it seemed past all belief. He had read in one of Charlie Murphy's books of the marvellous gifts bestowed by fairies, and this seemed almost like a fairy story which would end in " living happy to the end of his days."

He whistled and sang from morning to night, he was so active at the shop, so polite to customers, so meek under all Mrs. Brian's rebukes, that she suddenly became quite sorry to part with him, and bribed him by a shilling a week extra to stay. A shilling ! no, not for twenty shillings every Saturday would Fluffy have given up the school-life which was coming. Was he not going to make his way, and do something far better than serving potatoes and cabbages, and measuring out pennyworths of nuts? as he said to Mrs. Murphy with glee, when he told of Mrs. Brian's offer.

"If you were to keep at a greengrocer's the rest of your life, Fluffy, you might do your duty there and please God. I don't myself like to hear boys and girls talk as if nothing was good enough for them. If our Blessed Lord could come down from heaven to work like a poor boy in the carpenter's shop, *we* have no reason to be above things."

"I thought you were glad I was going to school," said Fluffy.

"So I am, very glad. Don't you believe I want you to get on just as if you were my own boy? It isn't that—I'm thanking God from my heart that He has found you a friend, and you'll be taken out of temptation. You're sure to find it come in another way though, Fluffy—even at school with the priest looking after you."

"I haven't taken the old woman's things," said Fluffy, still not quite pleased with Mrs. Murphy.

"It isn't so much what you've done, lad," said Mrs. Murphy; "that's between you and God. *I* see you might have been more faithful—it is what you've left *un*done I'm thinking of, Fluffy. Come now, have you been as good as you might?"

"No," said Fluffy, colouring; then conquering his temper he added, "I think I'd got to feel as if it was enough so long as I was honest.

"Yes, that is the way with us all. We're so apt to think we're doing 'enough' when we keep out of grievous sin. That wasn't our Lord's way with us, Fluffy. He never said He'd done enough."

Fluffy wriggled uneasily on his chair and then began to whistle, but it was no use—there came over him such a sense of all he had left *un*done ; of the sins of temper, and of tongue, the waste of time, the hurried prayers, the giddy talk with other boys, that he could not put it away. It was then that the boy made the resolve which never left him in after years—the resolve to be *all* for God ; to give more duty, more love, more service than was really forced on him by the laws of the Church. In a word, Fluffy meant to be generous, and he prayed that he might be made so, though he put his desire in only simple and unlearned words.

He did not know much of what school-life would be, but he did know that there must, among a number, be boys who would laugh at his efforts to be good, and boys who perhaps, would tempt him away from what was right. He would have to be brave, he would have to stand up boldly for what was right and true, no matter what the consequences might be. Could he do it ? There came back to Fluffy the thought of how he had tried and prayed to be good before his first Communion. It had not seemed to him so very hard to fight against his evil nature when it was fighting to win that great grace. Oh how he had resolved, and oh how he had promised God never, never to be his old sinful self, and yet—well, he had not been faithful, he had grown weary of the struggle, he had not taken care of the treasure which had been given him—not done what he purposed when, lying in weakness on his bed, the God of heaven had come to be his Guest.

Fluffy felt more humble after that evening. Happy, he was still; pleased too with the prospect before him; full of bright anticipations, yet he grew quieter and more thoughtful as the day drew on for him to go away.

When Fluffy took his seat for the first time among his companions at the Boys' Orphanage, which was now to be his home, his eyes were bright with pleasure. All that he had been told of other boys who had worked their way upwards in the world, came back to him in that moment; it should not be want of work or want of will which hindered him—of that he was quite certain.

# CHAPTER XV.

EVERY morning as the postman passed down the street, Mrs. Murphy looked out for a letter from Fluffy. At last it came, and though written in a large scrawling hand he had evidently done his best.

"Dear Mrs. Murphy and Charlie" (thus it ran), "I hope you are quite well as, thank God, it leaves me at present. I like the school very well, and I mean to get on. Dear Mrs. Murphy, I hope you will soon write me a letter. Please tell Father Dunstan I am quite well, and that I mean to get on. There are a great many boys here. Dear Mrs. Murphy, I am thankful to you for all you have done for me, and I mean to be a good boy and get on; and please tell Father Dunstan I am thankful to him too, and mean to be a good boy. Please, Charlie, write to me soon, and hoping you are quite well, no more at present.

"From yours affectionately,
"JOHN DUNSTAN."

Then followed a verse of a hymn, evidently written to fill up the sheet. Nobody laughed over poor Fluffy's letter; with all its faults and corrections they liked to have it, and Mrs. Murphy put it carefully by in a large old rosewood work-box which had once belonged to her grandmother, and which contained a medley of treasures.

"That boy will turn out well, I know," she said when she had read the letter to her husband. "Now he is to get some schooling, I don't see anything to keep him from being a teacher by-and-by. He doesn't say much; but for all that I know how his mind is set on it."

"Boys change their minds often enough," said Murphy; "I wouldn't build too much on that notion if I were you. It's enough to know that Fluffy is well taken care of for a long while to come."

"I'm sure the place feels quite dull without him," Mrs. Murphy exclaimed after a short silence. "I never could have thought a poor boy out of the street who is nothing to me any more than hundreds like him, could have got to feel so like a lad of my own."

Charlie heard and he did not like it—he had heard it before, and he never *had* quite liked it. Now as he went down the street to school he was trying to make out

15

what there was to vex him in his mother's affection for Fluffy. Did he not care for the poor boy himself? did he not really wish to be his friend? Yes, Charlie was sure that he did.

It was a disagreeable idea, but come it would—the idea that what he felt must really be some faint spark of jealousy. As long as he could remember, there had been no one but himself for his mother to have and care for; now, when he saw her sewing away for Fluffy, and when he heard her speak affectionately of him, a thrill shot through his heart as if something hurt him.

He was angry with himself for feeling so; he said, " I'm *not* jealous, *I* don't care;" but all the while he knew that he *did* care, and that the very "caring" was a sign of something wrong within. Charlie, with all his good points of character, had a fiery temper, and

now it seemed as if he could not conquer it—
"could not" because he did not pray for help.

Everything went amiss—even to the
sums, which were usually a great success
with him, and at last, as one of the boys
made some sneering remark when they were
all rushing out together, Charlie, beside himself with temper and wounded pride, struck
the offender several heavy blows. A sense
of shame crept over him in a moment, and
taking to his heels he was off and on his
way home. Mrs. Murphy was there to meet
him, but for the first time her boy pushed
rudely past her, and dashed upstairs to his
own small room.

*He* had done this; he, the model boy of
the school, the boy of whom priests and
teachers spoke so well—Charlie rocked himself to and fro in the misery of the thought.
As he sat cowering there, it seemed as if the

boy was living over again all his life, and instead of finding it fair and good, it was full of selfishness and pride. He tried to imagine himself aggrieved by his mother, by his master, by every one—even poor Fluffy— but it would not do with a conscience as keen as his. It was pride which had brought about his fall, and Charlie Murphy knew it. As he sat there he remembered how often, when Fluffy had got into trouble for some of his careless, giddy nonsense while he was at Mrs. Brian's, he had judged the boy severely, and felt a sort of contempt for his idle, thoughtless ways, which was always accompanied by an approving reflection upon himself.

Now, with his own self-respect broken down, Charlie could see again the frank expression of Fluffy's face as he owned to his faults, could understand better how

humble of heart was the poor, friendless
lad who never thought well of himself, or
wished to be highly spoken of.  Ah ! it was
the old, old fault which had come up under
a new shape and form.  What should he
do with it ?  Would it be nothing more
than fighting and failing ?  Was it not as
well to give up, and not aim at being good ?
Such were the thoughts which came crowding
upon Charlie then, but happily other thoughts
came too.  He did not know why, but in the
struggle he suddenly thought of one of the
parables of the New Testament—the parable
of the Prodigal Son, who, when he had
found out the very worst of his sins and
miseries, thought of the Father whom he
had offended.  Sinful, undutiful, as he had
been, he determined to return and repent—
not to turn away and become worse until all
was lost.  Here was Charlie's example.  A

depth of evil and misery indeed he had found within him—pride, selfishness, and many more faults. But should he turn from God because of these things—from God, Who only could make him better and purer? Humbled and ashamed, Charlie went quietly out of the house to find Father Dunstan, and laying all his burden down at the feet of Christ, he went back to his mother, "her own boy once more," as she said.

It seemed to Charlie after that, as if he must be always doing something kind to Fluffy, just as if he had suffered from his unkind thoughts. Every Sunday he would sit down to write a long letter of news—news of the church, and of Father Dunstan, of "mother," "father," and himself, yes, even of the old tabby cat whose feet Fluffy had once encased in walnut-shells, though he was very fond of her too.

These letters were the great delight of poor Fluffy's life at that time. With all his desire to get on, he did not find it easy, and there were moments when, in his utter weariness of reading, writing, and sums, he could *almost* have wished himself back in the streets; but if such gloomy feelings came, they were all dispersed by news from "home," as he called it. No—he wasn't going to disappoint them, let it be ever so hard to learn; so Fluffy's lessons always went on more satisfactorily both to himself and his teachers after the receipt of one of Charlie's letters.

Months passed by; winter was gone again, and spring had come—Fluffy's first spring in the country. To the little London-reared fellow, it was wonderful to see the budding trees and flowers, to hear the birds singing in the branches. Once

Granny Ward had kept a blackbird in a wicker cage, but only for a week or two, and its melancholy, captive note had been all Fluffy's experience in the matter of bird voices. There were games out of doors, and long walks for the school-boys; in fact, it was a time which Fluffy always remembered to the end of his life with pleasure—a pleasure which quite swallowed up any recollection of difficulties and scrapes, which doubtless came on some of the days.

It was during that spring, that one day visitors came to see the school, and though this was no rare occurrence, Fluffy seemed to take an unusual interest in one of the two gentlemen who stood looking on at the games in the play-ground. Where had he seen that quiet but kind face? Fluffy's respectable acquaintances had been so very few that it seemed scarcely possible he should know any one that was likely to come there, and yet he felt sure he did. Suddenly, a movement of the head reminded him of the prison chaplain—of Mr. Morton. Yes, it was he, it *must* be he, and without a moment's hesitation he quitted his companions and ran up to where the two gentlemen stood talking with Father Jackson.

"Oh sir, oh Mr. Morton!" he cried. "I thought I'd never see you again, and I *am* so glad. Don't you remember me, sir—Fluffy, as I was called?"

"John Dunstan!" said Father Jackson, surprised—"Fluffy!" exclaimed Mr. Morton, both together.

"Yes, sir, Fluffy," said the boy, speaking very fast and lowering his tone with a glance towards the group he had left. "I was in the prison, sir—Father Jackson, he knows, but I don't want the boys to hear. Number

67, sir, I was, and you told me about the Lord Jesus Christ, and made me want to be a good boy. Don't you remember, sir, how I promised when my time was up I'd never be a thief again? and I've kept my word, thank God for it, and now I'm here," and at this point Fluffy's breath failed him.

He was not mistaken, it was Mr. Morton, once—though no longer—the prison chaplain. As he looked at the eager, blushing face before him he knew it again, though so great a change had passed over it.

" My boy, I too am glad to see you once more. I remember you now, indeed, I have never forgotten your story, but I see so many lads, that for a moment you puzzled me, nor did I expect to find you here. Why Fluffy, how did you come to a Catholic school?"

" Ah, it does seem a strange thing," said Fluffy. " I'll tell you, sir, all that's happened since I saw you," and sitting in a quiet room where Father Jackson had sent him for a talk with his former friend, the boy told of how he had been helped and cared for since he left the prison.

"It is wonderful," said Mr. Morton earnestly. "God has indeed been very good to you, and I hope you love Him in return."

"I do try," said Fluffy shyly.

The clergyman rose and paced up and down the room as if there was something he wished, and yet scarcely liked, to say.

"My dear boy," he said at last, "I am sure you have found very good friends, friends to whom you must be grateful all your life. I do not want to make you forgetful of all they have done, but perhaps you are old enough to understand that I, as a clergyman of the Church of England, cannot feel satisfied to know you are being trained as a Catholic. Do you know that there are other forms of religion besides that which you are following?"

He tried to put the question simply, and yet the words seemed not those which could convey his meaning to a little unlearned boy —it surprised him then to see Fluffy's intelligent face. "Oh I know there's a lot of make-believe religions, sir, as I may say. There's only ours which is real and true."

"Of course you are taught so," replied Mr. Morton gravely. "I am not a Catholic, Fluffy; do you think my religion is a make-believe?"

For a moment the boyish face was troubled, but the answer came steadily; "I *know* it is, sir, if you don't belong to the Catholic Church."

Mr. Morton smiled. "You have got your lesson perfectly I see, but you may learn others. Do you remember, Fluffy, when I first told you of the Saviour—of Christ Jesus Who died for you? You believed me then; try and believe now that I want to see you belonging to Him, and a member of His Church. Don't you *want* to belong to Him, Fluffy?"

"Oh, sir—Mr. Morton," said Fluffy, colouring very much. "I don't rightly know how to say it; if I'm rude or ungrateful to you who was once so kind, I beg you to pardon me. This is what I want to say, sir. That I think I *do* belong to Him more than you do, though I'm sure you're very good as far as you know how, and I'm only trying. I mean that Christ's Church is the Catholic Church, and no other, and I'm in it now, so I know I belong to Him."

Mr. Morton sighed; he could argue against Catholicism with educated people, but he seemed beaten down by this boy's simple and unlearned faith.

"I am sure there are many good, excellent Catholics who really wish to serve God, but they are in error, Fluffy, and I want to get you out of it."

The boy shook his head. "I couldn't believe any religion but my own, sir. We've got our Lord with us always, and you haven't."

"You do not know what you say," replied Mr. Morton. "You are only a young lad, and you cannot judge rightly. Oh, Fluffy, I am asking you to give up all your images, and candles, and flowers which please your eye, but lead your thoughts away from God—from Jesus Christ, Whom I told you of in the old prison days."

"I haven't forgotten those days," said Fluffy, with a far-away look in his eyes, as if he was gazing once more at the walls of his cell, or at Mr. Morton's kind face when he talked to him there and cheered him on with hope of a better future. "Over and over again I've told Father Dunstan about you, and how you were the very first to tell me about our Blessed Lord ; but oh, sir, you didn't tell me enough ! You told me to believe He could forgive me, but you never told me that He was waiting to wash away my sins with His precious Blood. You never told me that if I confessed them, He'd pardon all and make my soul white and pure. And, Mr. Morton, you told me how Christ Jesus lived in heaven and saw me always, but you didn't ever say how He lived on earth too. You haven't got Him in your churches, so I suppose you don't rightly know what it's like to go and kneel before Him and know He isn't only away up in heaven, but there, quite near, looking, and listening, and loving."

There was a great silence; then, as a distant bell rang, Fluffy rose up. "I'll have to go now, sir; I'm so glad I've seen you, and I hope some day you'll come again. And if I've said anything you don't like, I hope it's no offence; but oh, Mr. Morton, if ever you find a boy as poor and bad and ignorant as me, please tell him *all*. You don't know how it would help him!"

The clergyman held out his hand. "I hope I shall see you again, Fluffy, for I live not so very many miles from here. I shall pray very much for you, and you—well, I should like you to pray for me."

"Oh, I do," said Fluffy brightly. "I say three Hail Marys for you every day that you may be converted. Good-bye, sir—good-bye."

# CHAPTER XVI.

MR. MORTON's young brother found him a very dull companion as they went away from their visit to the Catholic school.

"I cannot get the words of that boy out of my head," he said, in explanation of his long fits of silence.

"What, that bright-eyed little chap who came up and claimed your acquaintance? I thought you were never going to end your private conversation."

"I was very glad to talk with the boy for a bit. I am almost surprised the priest let me see him alone."

"Oh, he was showing me the place," said

16

George Morton. "Besides, I don't suppose he was afraid you'd do the little fellow any harm. I must say that Catholics don't seem to fear us for their children as we do them; they feel so sure, I suppose, that their faith is well rooted in."

The clergyman made no direct reply, but appeared rather to be following the course of his own thoughts, for presently he said :

"That boy was once at the prison during my chaplaincy, a little, ignorant 'gutter-lad.' I remember how the story of Christ's life and death seemed to sink into him; he never appeared to be tired of listening, and now he tells me he remembers it all—only I did not tell him ' enough.' "

" A wonderful appetite for good things," said the younger man lightly, but his brother frowned on him.

"I dislike such remarks, George. What

I meant was that this boy, this poor Fluffy, is convinced that I told him truly, but that it did not go far enough—his religion has supplied the rest. I wonder if this is so with all who go over to the Church of Rome—not so much the giving up of any received article of·faith, as an addition and expansion of belief."

He sighed again, and looked puzzled, and after awhile the brothers talked of other things; but for long months Fluffy's simple words haunted the clergyman, while, away in his school, the boy's prayers were still offered for the conversion of his first friend.

Fluffy sometimes wondered why Mr. Morton did not keep his promise, and pay a second visit to the school; it was years after that he knew his prayers had not been in vain, and that away in a foreign land, to

which he had gone, Mr. Morton's heart opened
at last to receive the truth which had won the
poor street boy, and he became a member of
the Church of Christ, and afterwards a
zealous and holy priest.

Fluffy often wished he could write and
tell Father Dunstan about that meeting,
during the months when it remained freshly
and strongly in his mind; but he was slow
in composing and completing a letter, and
then there was not so very much time, and
so the remembrance of it all gradually
faded, only to be recalled when—long years
after—he met Mr. Morton again.

As he became more used to school and
to study, Fluffy grew reconciled to all that
had at first seemed hard, and he applied
himself so closely that he rose quickly to a
good place among his fellows.

He was bright and lively at play, but,

could he choose, the greatest of all happiness was reading. Books of every kind were welcome, but such as told of the success of those who were born in lowly circumstances were his especial delight. One day he lighted on the story of Dick Whittington, and it seemed almost as if he had met a friend ; he saw again in fancy Mrs. Murphy's bright kitchen, the neatly spread table round which they sat, as Mr. Murphy told of the message the bells had rung out to the weary orphan boy on Highgate roadway. And then he remembered what Mrs. Murphy had said he ought to fancy the church bells told *him.* "A schoolmaster !" oh, would it really and truly come about ? Not quite so improbable, now, perhaps, as when he had first felt the desire, and yet almost more than he could hope to attain. Still he did hope, nay, he even prayed for it. Truly, as Mr. Murphy had once said, boys are changeful in their dreams and desires, but Fluffy never swerved from his; and, as it grew and strengthened, he found courage to speak of it to one of the priests who had charge of the orphanage. Once possessed of this knowledge of Fluffy's constant thought, Father Jackson set himself to find out what were the boy's capabilities for such a work. Sometimes he was put as monitor over a class of younger boys, and his happiness, his patience, his interest in his business went far to convince the priest that teaching was to be God's work for Fluffy—his vocation.

When the boy knew this, the dreams and desires became a steady purpose which spurred him on in his own education, and, better still—animated him to try to be very generous with God. Well was it that Fluffy had always seemed to understand that he never could be fit, *really* fit to teach others, unless he was living a good, Christian life. Well was it for him—and in later days for others—that he did not look upon the calling of a schoolmaster *only* as a means of securing a respectable livelihood. In the days when he had been very poor and ignorant he had grasped the truth which some, far better taught, far better trained, have missed seeing—that there must be personal piety, personal love of God, if he was to do any lasting good in such a position. He had not put the thought, perhaps, into quite this form when it had come to him as he served out sugar and sweets in the grocer's shop, or ran to and fro to Mrs. Murphy's little home; but he had often wondered whether he could ever be half "good enough" to teach poor boys, ever love God so much that he could help them

to love Him too. Now, when he thought
it all over in quiet moments during the day,
or spoke of the hoped-for future with Father
Jackson, the same feeling was there.

"I am not good enough, not half worthy,"
he said in his humility of heart; but then
there came a sure, strong promise of help,
the promise once given to the apostle of
whom Father Dunstan had told him, "My
grace is sufficient for thee."

There would be no real humility in doubt-
ing that strength and that grace. Fluffy
knew it; when the time came for him to
begin his work, it would be given him.

Much as the boy thought of all these
things, his schoolmates had no idea that
anything serious was in his mind; they only
knew he was always good-natured, always
forgiving, always regular in the duties of
school, as he was faithful and regular in his

religious duties. There were boys in that school who were acknowledged "good," but still were disagreeable to their companions in many ways—Fluffy was not so, just because he was humble, and did not perceive his own virtues.

He had read many of the lives of God's most holy servants, but perhaps it was the life of the Blessed John Berchmans which he best liked, because it was so full of such simple ways of goodness. He found there, that John was a cheerful merry boy, but he also read that he watched carefully over his words, lest God might be offended—here was a lesson for himself. He found also that Berchmans bore unkindness without vexation or complaint, that he loved lowly offices, that he never showed taste for special kinds of food or murmured at what was set before him, and what were these and others

but simple everyday virtues which any boy
might practise, and yet which by God's
grace would make a good and noble life.
*Any boy*, did I say? Yes, Fluffy felt that
it was so, and that even he might imitate
the blessed servant of God of whom he
loved to read, if only he tried in the same
way—the way of constant, humble prayer
to God and His Blessed Mother.

It is not surprising when Fluffy was
striving like this to be good, that excellent
reports of him were sent from time to time
to Father Dunstan, who passed them on to
Mrs. Murphy, thus causing her the greatest
delight.

"He always was a dear good boy, yes,
*always*, though he had his faults and trying
ways like all the rest." That was what she
would say to her husband and Charlie. And
he?—well he was fighting so hard against his

nature that he really began to feel a true, honest pleasure in hearing Fluffy praised, and it was a pleasure which increased as he strove to feel it one.

"We may all learn a lesson from Fluffy, I think," Father Dunstan said one day. "It seems to me that he has set to work to be 'faithful in little,' and if we also are that, there is good reason to hope we shall be also faithful in greater things when they come."

"Faithful in little!" the words rang in Mrs. Murphy's ears as she bustled about her house and daily work, and oh! how well she tried to do it, yes, even down to the cleaning of her saucepans and the peeling of the potatoes.

"Faithful in little!" Murphy himself, good workman and sober husband as he had ever been, felt that the thought made him better; more careful to use every moment fully, more careful to do his best, because it was service for God.

"Faithful in little!" ah, I could not tell you how the words kept Charlie back from small faults, or how they encouraged him on in small duties. Father Dunstan had always liked and always esteemed the boy, but he could have told you better than I how—after that great humbling view of self, of which you have already heard — Charlie Murphy seemed to "grow" in the love and in the service of God.

So to each one in different ways the tidings of Fluffy's good conduct was doing real benefit—it even encouraged Father Dunstan in moments when mind and body were weary and depressed with the sight of misery and sin which seemed so hard to help and combat.

If any one had journeyed to the boys' orphanage and whispered to Fluffy that his example was doing good to others, that he had been even a little help to those who he knew were better and wiser than himself, how surprised he would have been! But God does not often let us know these things —it would be so very hard to know them and still keep humble. Only in the last day, when the secrets of all hearts shall be revealed, we too shall know what we have done for God by example and by influence. Alas! only then shall we fully understand what we *might* have done, yet did not.

# CHAPTER XVII.

THOUGH at times, days and weeks drag slowly by, years seem past and gone like a dream when we look back—just as our old friend Fluffy looked back when the morning came on which he could say it was fourteen years since he had made his first Communion. There is no one left in the little home to which Jesus in the Blessed Sacrament came then as a guest—the houses even have been cleared away, and larger, handsomer buildings erected in their place.

Yet Father Dunstan is labouring for the people he has dwelt amongst so long, and still he numbers in his congregation the

Murphys, who, with their son, live only a short walk from the Catholic Church.

Charlie's early hopes are realised now. He has risen steadily from one step to another in the ladder of success until he occupies a responsible and well-paid situation in one of the large mercantile houses of the City. He has a pretty and comfortable home now for his parents; better even than he dreamed of in his boyish days.

No more need for his father to go out to his work from early morning till late night. He could not be happy if he did nothing after a life of activity and industry, but still it is not by his toil that the home must be kept going, and he can take short hours with a clear conscience and a quiet mind.

No need either for Mrs. Murphy to do any more household labour than she wishes —a neat, trim little maid is there to do her bidding, who seems likely to become a model servant under the eye of the good woman whom Katie can't help liking, even if she *does* confide sometimes to the girl next door when they are shaking the mats at the same moment that "the missis is a bit of a fidget." And then, though Charlie is not apt to tell his secrets, his father and mother smile well-pleased as they speak of the time—drawing very near—when he is going to bring home a good Catholic wife, who will be a daughter to them in their old age, and a help and comfort to her husband when *they* are gone.

And Fluffy——

Well, come to another part of London where we have taken you before in our story of his life. Go but a few minutes' distance from quiet streets and gentlemen's houses, and you will find yourself (if you take the right turnings) in Dockett's-buildings, apparently as miserable and bad as it was years ago. Yet even there some slight gleam of light has entered, for a Catholic Church stands hardly more than a stone's throw from the court, and many a time the priest has made his way to those dirty dwellings to search for souls which once, perhaps, were God's, but now are dead in sin.

Some of the children come to the Catholic school, and if you ask any boy amongst them what is the name of the schoolmaster, he will tell you, " Mr. Dunstan."

It was one August day that Fluffy entered on his work there after the toil and preparation of fourteen years. You would not know him in the quiet, but pleasant-looking man, whose bright eyes seem to glance into every corner of the school-room, and into the corners even of the boys' hearts.

17

I could never tell you how he loves his work—to him it is as real a vocation as the vocation of a priest, though of a lower degree. It is God's place for him, God's work with which he is intrusted, and as he looks round upon his scholars each morning, he tries always to remember what Father Dunstan told him so long ago—to be faithful, to be earnest, as if his Master was visibly by his side.

With such a thought, it is not strange that he has gained such power over the once unruly boys—how can he be hasty, unjust, impatient, when he sees in every child one who is to be lost, or won for God? one for whom *he* must account as far as his influence has gone to affect that child's future?

And so it is that Mr. Dunstan the school-master is loved and respected by his boys, and that he wins his way with many of their parents. Working hard all day, he yet has leisure moments, and at such times there is nothing he likes so well as to turn into Dockett's-buildings, perhaps to look after a truant, perhaps to see a sick boy, but *always* to get in a word for God. No one lives there now whom he once knew; Granny Ward has long been dead, and her name scarcely remembered, but still the footway swarms with half-clothed children, and the houses are full to overflowing with their untidy and intemperate parents. It is a well-known fact that there are those who, refusing to admit the priest, will be civil to the schoolmaster; but then it is equally well known that sooner or later Mr. Dunstan can persuade them to open their doors to Father Wallace, and thus not unfrequently some soul is brought back to the feet of Christ.

One evening when he had several visits to

17—2

pay in Dockett's-buildings, the schoolmaster
was told of a fresh arrival, an old broken-
down man who seemed to know the place,
but whom none there knew, who had established himself in an attic in one of the
houses " to die,"as he said.

Mr. Dunstan went to him there, to find
him apparently ill and utterly alone—so ill
and so desolate that he seemed to welcome
a visitor.  Slowly and painfully he told his
story—yes, he had lived there before, "years
and years back—him and poor Polly and
the little un."

Being asked if he had no friends to
attend to him now he was so ill, he covered
his face with his hands, and a half-groan
broke from him.

" Never a one, never a one," he gasped.
" I might have had.  I had a decent wife
once, aye, and a decent home, and I dragged

her down to misery, and then I left her—
her and the little un.  She's dead now, I'm
thinking, for she were a poor ailing thing.
I shan't ever see her no more, but sometimes
I wishes as I could get tidings of the boy—
he *were* a knowing little chap, were Fluffy."

"What name did you say?" but the
voice was quiet, even if Mr. Dunstan's heart
throbbed wildly.

"Fluffy, we used to call him.  It wasn't
his name—his name were Alfred—only I
took to calling him so when he were a baby,
'cause he were such a funny-looking little
chap with his hair all fluffy and sticking out
all ways, like a crow's nest.  He'd be a man
now, would Fluffy."

"Were you married at church? and the
child, was he baptised?"

"That's the same as christened, isn't it,
mister?  No, I wouldn't have none of that,

though poor Polly, she cried and most broke her heart about it. You see, I'd took her from her church and her tidy ways till she'd given up heart altogether for herself, but somehow when the child were born, she'd set her mind to have him christened, and we'd a hard fight over it, and at last she give in."

"Where were you married?"

"Away in the city. She were a Catholic, were Polly. Not a born one, but turned to it through being a servant with Catholics. So we was married at one of her churches; you may find our names writ down in a big book, 'John Haines and Mary Elford,' away up at Moorfields it were."

The man stopped, and leaned back his head against the bundle which was his pillow; so much speaking had exhausted him, and for some minutes he lay with closed eyes.

Then opening them, and looking at his visitor, he spoke again.

"It's hard to lie here a-dying, and not a wife nor a child to look to me, isn't it, mister? My own fault, too, my own fault, like all the rest of it. Polly might have been alive now, and the boy growed up to be a comfort to me, if I hadn't been what I have."

"Did you ever hear of God, and of Christ?" said the schoolmaster, bending down to catch the answer. When it came, the voice was lower than before, lower and more troubled.

"Aye, that I have—years and years agone, when I were a little fellow no bigger than Fluffy were when I left him. I were taught about God then, but I've been too bad for Him to look at me now."

"But you know—you *must* know if you

have ever heard of Christ, that He came to pardon sin, to love sinners."

"Aye, I've heard that too, but I tell you I've been too bad for Him to pardon me, and I'm dying—there's no time left."

"Would it comfort you to hear that Fluffy is living—living, and well and happy, too?"

"Comfort me! ah, I should think so! Poor little chap! Perhaps you've heard of him, mister? perhaps you've lived in this part years gone by?" And he looked wistfully at the kind face of Mr. Dunstan.

"Father"—and he took the rough, hard hand in his—"Father, I am your own boy; I am Fluffy."

"You?—*you* Fluffy? Why, I can't believe as he could have growed up such a one to look at, and yet—well, there's a kind of light in your eyes that calls to mind poor Polly. You're not making fun of a dying man ?"

For answer, John Dunstan in a few words told the story of his life, of his mother's death, and his own misery, but later of his happiness.

" And now, father, would you do me one favour—just promise me one thing because I am your own Fluffy."

" I'd promise you a thousand, if I could do 'em."

" It is only this, father. Let me bring to you one of God's priests ; tell him your sins, and let him in Christ's name give you pardon before you die. Die in the Catholic Church, father; it is the only safe way."

Long did Fluffy plead, but at length his request was granted, and he hastened to seek the priest, thinking as he went of the

wonderful goodness of God in bringing
about such a meeting. His mother had
been a Catholic, then! Oh, how did she
die? Was there one fervent act of sorrow,
one cry to Jesus and Mary? He could
only leave it all to God. But there was his
father, who might still be rescued from
eternal death. What a happiness was that!"

In less than a quarter of an hour the
people in Dockett's-buildings saw both
priest and schoolmaster go into the house
where the strange man lay dying.

Life was ebbing very fast now—Father
Wallace saw it, and taking water, baptised
him; then, kneeling down by his side, spoke
earnestly. What he said, John could imagine
by his dying father's answer.

· "Sorry—yes, I'm sorry for 'em all. I'd
do very different if I'd my time over again.
Tell 'em all?—yes. I'd do that, and glad

if so be I could get 'em washed away. I've heard it years agone. I somehow always b'lieved it, too, only I thought I'd wait a bit. Yes, and now there's no time. I'm going fast."

Very slowly and distinctly the priest said an Act of Contrition, which the man repeated after him with some difficulty, pausing frequently for breath.

Suddenly a convulsive movement passed through him, his eyes closed, and a change came over his face.

"Jesus, mercy! Mary, help!" said Father Wallace.

Once he had uttered it; at the second time the dying man tried to speak the words, and thus trying he passed away into God's presence.

"Trust our Lord with it all," said Father Wallace to his schoolmaster. "It is not for us to measure a man's repentance, and surely none ever cried to Jesus and Mary in vain."

When the stranger's coffin was carried from the poor lodging which had sheltered his last days, the people of Dockett's-buildings ran out to look after it, and saw Mr. Dunstan, the schoolmaster, following it to the grave. No one wondered why, for it was so like him to do a deed of charity and kindness, and they all knew that he had been with the poor dead man at the last; it never would have come into their minds to imagine that it was a son burying his long-lost father.

To his priest, to Father Dunstan, and the Murphys only is it known that the schoolmaster, whose heart seems to warm most to the poorest and lowest of his boys, was once as dirty; as poor, as friendless as any one of them ; even one of the little urchins of Dockett's-buildings, who knew no other name than " Fluffy."

THE END.